COW BOYHOOD

Thirteen-year-old Wilder has spent his boyhood watching men like his grandpa Papa Milam ... and wanting to be like them. Now he is leaving on a two-day cattle drive through river and canyon country with his aging Papa and another older man, Red Guffey. In big ranch country full of livestock and wild animals, Wilder is forced to recognize that his own instincts and abilities may have become greater than those of his heroes.

The Adventures of
Wilder Good

#1 *The Elk Hunt: The Adventure Begins*

Finalist, Lamplighter 2016 Triple Crown Awards

"If you like Hank, you'll like Wilder Good too."
—John R. Erickson, author of *Hank the Cowdog*

"Among the best books for young boys I've seen
in years. This is classic Americana, values and all."
—Robert Pratt, *Pratt on Texas*

#2 *Texas Grit*

Winner, 2015 Will Rogers Gold Medallion Award
for Young Readers

"I am a big fan of this series. *Texas Grit* is every
bit as insightful and positive as the first one."
—Glenn Dromgoole, *Texas Reads*

"Dahlstrom writes about ranch life with flair and specific
detail." —WORLD magazine

#3 *Wilder and Sunny*

Finalist, Lamplighter 2017 Triple Crown Awards

"These are exciting tales . . . Dahlstrom's superb writing
takes Wilder through those anxiety-producing years
between childhood and adulthood, when life's simplest and
most important lessons are learned." —*Forbes*

#4 *The Green Colt*

Winner, 2017 Wrangler Western Heritage Award for Juvenile Book

Winner, 2017 Will Rogers Gold Medallion Award
for Young Readers

Finalist, 2017 Western Writers of America Spur Award
for Juvenile Fiction

Finalist, Lamplighter 2018 Triple Crown Awards

"*The Green Colt* is told beautifully, with grace and quiet power, and shows S. J. Dahlstrom to be a big new talent. I highly recommend this wonderful book." —Nancy Plain, award-winning author and vice-president of Western Writers of America

#5 *Black Rock Brothers*

Finalist, 2019 Will Rogers Gold Medallion Award for Young Readers

"The story will hook adventure-loving boys while delighting parents with its character-building plot." —WORLD magazine

"It's a rewarding journey for anyone, and may just inspire some enterprising boy to put down the PlayStation and start dreaming of his own quest." —*Redeemed Reader*

#6 *Silverbelly*

Winner, 2021 Wrangler Western Heritage Award for Juvenile Book

Winner, 2020 Will Rogers Gold Medallion Award for Young Readers

Finalist, 2021 Western Writers of America Spur Award for Juvenile Fiction

"Sometimes you learn nature's lessons by hearing them, and sometimes you learn them by experience. There is no better author writing today describing both." —Will Rogers Medallion Award committee

"Anyone who eats meat should read this book." —*The Slatonite*

"Spur Award finalist S.J. Dahlstrom has brought this coming-of-age tale to life through his natural, easy writing style and stunningly beautiful descriptions. I have been a Wilder fan from the start, and each subsequent adventure only gets better." —*Roundup Magazine*

#7 *Cow Boyhood*

#**7**

The Adventures of
Wilder Good

COW BOYHOOD

S. J. DAHLSTROM

Illustrations by Cliff Wilke

PAUL DRY BOOKS
Philadelphia 2021

First Paul Dry Books Edition, 2021

Paul Dry Books, Inc.
Philadelphia, Pennsylvania
www.pauldrybooks.com

Copyright © 2021 S. J. Dahlstrom
All rights reserved

Printed in the United States of America

Library of Congress Control Number: 2021939922

ISBN-13: 978-1-58988-154-9

CONTENTS

for my compadres at Whetstone—
past, present, future—
keepers of the code

I had to go. It was my last chance to be a boy.

—Theodore Roosevelt, 1914, concerning his trip
  down an unknown river in the Amazon

*We also held the common knowledge that we were
tough. . . . Perhaps we always wondered which of us was
tougher, but, if boyhood questions aren't answered before
a certain point in time, they can't ever be raised again.*

—A River Runs Through It by Norman Maclean

*That old man speaking you have heard
since your boyhood, since his prime, his voice
speaking out of lives long dead, their minds
speaking in his own, by winter fires, in fields and woods,
in barns while the rain beat on roofs
and wind shook the girders. Stay and listen
until he dies or you die, for death
is in this, and grief is in it. Live here
as one who knows these things. Stay, if you live;
listen and answer. Listen to the next one
like him, if there is to be one.
Be the next one like him . . .*

—"The Record," a poem by Wendell Berry

CHAPTER ONE
Old Men

"I'm going to get me a buzzard," Red said to no one as he mashed the gas on his new, white turbo-diesel. Wilder was seated between two old men with failing eyesight. On the boy's right, Papa squinted.

Wilder could see the mass of large black birds conferencing around a smeared roadkill half a mile down the one lane Texas blacktop. He had some idea what "get me a buzzard" meant but he wasn't entirely sure his hunch was correct. As he had known them, old men like Red weren't foolish. But it appeared he was accelerating toward the wake of buzzards as if to hit one with the pickup. He knew there wasn't a chance to actually catch one.

Besides, who would want a buzzard anyway.

Wilder looked over at Papa as he often did in these unusual ranch situations. He knew better than to speak up unless an emergency was in progress or had been completed in all its bloody glory. Papa had a smirk on his gray-whiskered face, squinting through dark sunglasses under his cowboy hat.

The old man felt Wilder's gaze as the truck hit 85. The steel cow-catcher mounted on the front bumper whistled through the hot, summer air.

"They'll fly," he said, "Red couldn't hit a dead bird with a shovel."

Red mashed the gas pedal harder.

Wilder didn't think he had ever been this fast in a vehicle before. He glanced back over at the speedometer. The red line waved past 90. He always thought fast would be good, but this made his stomach flutter.

The buzzards were 100 yards away now and two on the side of the dinner circle closest to the pickup turned toward the vehicle and spread their wings. It looked like the others were still guzzling a smallish wild pig.

OK, surely we're going to slow down soon . . . Wilder thought.

Red stared ahead, looking like chubby kid in the candy store. His pale skin was covered with reddish freckles that blended into red and white short-cut hair under his hat. His large belly cascaded over his belt inches from the steering wheel, which he handled with his right hand from the bottom. The other arm was on the window sill, curly red hand hair flowing back in the wind.

The birds will move. The birds will move. Wilder chanted under his breath as he tightened his seat belt.

Three buzzards began to flap as the truck bore down on them. The lone vehicle roared through big ranch country in the steamy summer silence as if a bank had just been robbed. The whole scene was sent into fast-forward for the last 50 yards. Three birds remained, but seemed to panic.

"Red!!!" Papa yelled as he pulled his hat over his face and ducked.

Wilder saw the first three birds clear the road, but the last three were just getting airborne as he also ducked into the dash and covered his head. He heard Red slip a cussword out as the brakes screeched.

He heard a couple thumps and then he heard glass shatter.

Broken glass splashed all over Wilder and he felt something heavy tumble down his back and wedge between him and the seat back. Then an other-worldly stink surrounded him as he felt the pickup bounce to a fish-tail stop in the bar ditch as Red said, "Whoa, whoa, whoa," as if he were horseback. A dust cloud rose and billowed over them. Wilder tried to breathe but sucking in air was like drinking from the sewer. He raised up slowly and tiny glass crystals fell around him like clear water. He looked over at Papa.

He had blood across his face. There was a tiny piece of buzzard intestine hanging from his earlobe. He didn't appear dead, or mad. Kind of stunned. Wilder had never seen Papa stunned. The three of them looked out the front window through open air. A Hereford bull stared at the strange humans across the roadside fence line.

"Well, that ain't what I expected," Wilder heard Red say, making a third stunned person in the cab of the partially wrecked pickup.

"What *did* you expect?" Papa said in return, coolly.

Red ignored him.

"Wilder, you OK, son?" Red asked and followed with, "We better clear out of here."

Wilder nodded not wanting to open his mouth as he unbuckled and felt the wetness of the putrid and now pulverized buzzard fall off his back and sink into the fibers and cushions of Red's new pickup.

At the back of the pickup Red looked green and said he thought the buzzards were having pork, well done, and Wilder felt a wave pass over him that ended in a gasping vomit into the wildflowers. His hands gripped his knees, but he stayed on his feet. As he was spitting he mumbled, "I think we got two."

Then he saw Red follow in chain reaction, one hand on the pickup bed and other bracing his rotund stomach. Wilder had never heard an old man throw up before. It kind of sounded like he was dying.

Papa laughed as he slung globs of exploded buzzard off his clothes and onto the puking Red, his oldest buddy. "I don't reckon we'll try that again," he said to no one.

CHAPTER TWO
Ladders

The morning after the tragic pickup ride Wilder realized Papa had never been very interested in home repair. The old ranch house was in good shape, but that was mainly because Papa's wife Marian had handled it. She would call Larry in Amarillo and he would come out and replace windows, or re-grout stone and brick, or repair the roof when needed. Papa loved cows and horses and grass.

But Marian had passed nine years ago.

So Wilder knew the growing brown spots on the ceiling around the stone chimney weren't going to fix themselves. He had been watching them grow and morph into shapes that at one point resembled a giraffe, and then a forest, and then an aloe vera plant as he spent the summer before his freshman year of high school on the ranch in the panhandle of Texas. It had rained off and on all week. He didn't know if Papa had been noticing.

Wilder liked to work with his hands, and his dad, Hank, was a carpenter. They lived in a well-maintained trailer house, but Hank had trained Wilder to do about anything with tools. Wilder didn't want to tell his Papa his business, but he figured the old man would appreciate it. They had grown close the last two years. Wilder decided to ask.

"Papa, you want me to take a look at the roof? That sheet rock has been getting more soggy all week."

Papa looked up from his bill paying table and nodded. At 76, he had a limited sense of focus. To him, the house didn't matter much until something was on fire. He'd seen Wilder come through many times in tough circumstances so he figured the boy could handle the roof. Besides, it was something he hated messing with. He nodded agreement and went back to writing various checks. Papa's blue heeler dog, Coffee, hopped up from her master's feet and followed Wilder out of the house.

Coffee had cancer. It was plain to see by the growths on the old dog's right hind leg and back and a small tumor on the right side of her chest. She still moved naturally, despite the handicaps, and even took interest in nipping the heels of cows when alongside mounted cowboys. Papa never considered taking the dog for any surgery or expensive treatment. Veterinarians were for emergencies with livestock and the rare occasions when he couldn't figure out a horse or cow ailment on his own. With Papa's experience those circumstances were very few.

Wilder knew this too, and he scratched Coffee on the ears and neck and felt for ticks like he always had. The dog grunted her thanks and Wilder smiled. Dogs, he supposed, knew the deal—they would be loved and treated better than any other animal while they lived, but they were still animals. When their time came to go to the big front porch in the sky, they would go without a lot of fussy end-of-life care. It would still be clean and honest, like their cousins, the wolves and coyotes.

Coffee at his heels, Wilder went to the barn and rummaged up a ladder and dragged it to the front of the house. The oldest part of the house had been built on carved caprock blocks almost a hundred years before. The house had spread out since then with minor additions. The porch level was several feet off the ground and the roof line ten feet above that. The pitch was steep, giving the house an old fashioned attic, so the climb was no cake walk.

Used to modern, over-built ladders, Wilder grimaced at the old wooden one he was using. There was no telling how many years it had on it. Hank would have thrown it in the garbage. It creaked, step by step, as Wilder ascended. Wilder crested the roof and realized his cowboy boots were the wrong shoes. He took two steps and the asphalt shingles slid under him like roller skates. He creaked back down and changed into his moccasins.

The soft leather-bottomed shoes gripped better and he slipped up the valleys and over the peak to the back of the house where the chimney poked through the roof. He heard a pickup pull up and a door slam at the front of the house.

The old roof was rotten in several spots around the chimney, and the flashing and tar had pulled away from the stone. It wasn't going to be an easy job. It was past the point of patching, which Wilder could tell had been tried, probably by Papa, several times. He was going to have to tear some roof out and lay new sheathing, then re-shingle. It wasn't a complex job, but it wasn't fast either. Wilder took about ten minutes looking over the problem, making a mental list of the things he would need. Mainly supplies they would have to get in town.

He eased back over to the other side of the house and peeked over the ridge.

Papa was starting up the ladder. Papa's best friend, Red Guffey, was holding the ladder at the base. Wilder could barely see Papa's uncovered gray head and the cowboy hat and big belly of Red below him. On the third step of the ladder Wilder heard a crack and Papa and Red disappeared.

Wilder rushed over the peak and scrambled down to the edge. The two old men were in a pile on the ground. They weren't moving, yet. Wilder's eyes were wide, but he knew to keep quiet and not act stupid. They were men. They could handle it.

Red and Papa untangled and rolled onto their backs in the red mud from the recent rains. They puffed and stared up at the sky. Red's straw hat was flat and lay three feet away. Neither was in a hurry to right the ship.

"How much rain did you get this week?" Red finally spoke up.

"Three and seven-tenths."

"That ain't bad for all of summer."

"Yup."

They paused their talk and considered all their throbbing places and wondered if any were breaks, or worth mentioning.

"I haven't been bucked off in years, but I recall this is what it felt like," Red said.

"Yup."

"Grass stains and mud on your back. You think we should get up before the boy sees us?"

With that they both made groans and turned away from each other, went up to their knees, Papa standing first. He gave Red a hand up. He was much heavier. Red punched out his hat and started laughing. He brushed off Papa's backside for him and the favor was returned, although mud doesn't brush much.

Wilder waited another couple seconds before he made his appearance known. Papa had already remounted the ladder. Wilder spoke up.

"Papa, I checked it out. I know what we need."

Papa didn't look up. Red was back in position.

"Well, I'd better look at it."

Wilder was torn. He couldn't boss Papa, but this was not a good situation. The ladder was a joke, and Papa didn't look very good. Both old men might be hurt. That was no easy fall he had witnessed.

Papa went to the fourth rung, over-stepping the broken piece. That was a move Wilder might not have made, and he was 13. Wilder braced the top of the ladder and looked down in earnest. He tried again.

"Papa, I don't think this ladder is any good. I should have chosen a different one."

Papa just kept moving up. Rung by rung, Wilder waited for another crash. The ladder wobbled, but Red steadied it. Papa grunted. Wilder could see how thin his gray hair was on top. It looked like sparse lake weeds floating in the shallows.

He crested the roof line and looked almost surprised he had done it. Two more steps and he took Wilder's hand onto the incline.

"You watch it up there, Wendell," Red hollered.

"Red, I've been on this roof since I was five. I built most of it and have re-shingled it half a dozen times."

"Yeah, I know. That's why it's leaking like a chain link fence," Red chortled.

Papa and Wilder crawled over the roof, Wilder in the lead. At the chimney Wilder pointed out the rot. Papa put a hand on the old stone and breathed slowly . . . in and out.

"Papa, I'm not telling you what to do, but I can do this. You don't even have to come up again. We just need a town run and I'll knock it out."

Papa nodded.

On the way back over the ridge they sat on the peak for a breather, before facing the edge and the ladder again. They were 30 feet in the air and the caprock loomed over them and they loomed over the soapberry and cottonwood trees of the canyon. It wasn't hot yet at ten o'clock, but it was already getting there.

"Red wants to drive a bunch of cattle he just bought. They're in Turkey, about 20 miles from his ranch. He says we can do it in two days, spend one night out. Take them right down the river."

Wilder was amused. He knew he was being asked to go, or at the very least asked what he thought. That was kind of new. The old man wasn't in the habit of asking his advice about schedules or the cattle business.

"Why isn't he using cattle trucks to ship them?"

"I said the same thing. The job would be done in an hour."

Papa paused, looking at the caprock, and then at something past it, way off in the horizon. Wilder couldn't tell what it was.

"Well . . ." Wilder asked again.

"He said he's been wondering if he can still do it."

"Do what?"

"I'm not sure."

But Wilder knew. It was the question he had always been asking himself. *Can I do it?* He knew exactly what it meant. He was just surprised that Red was asking it.

And now, looking at Papa, he knew he was asking himself the same question.

They got off the roof without anybody dying.

ᗢ

CHAPTER THREE
Gearing Up

Josephine True Milam

Wilder didn't know what to think of Papa's wondering about Red's wondering about the drive. Like everything at the ranch, it seemed, he was excited and scared at the same time. He had learned that feeling meant it was something he needed to do.

He had just finished a ten-day backpacking trip with Big and Corndog back in Colorado and was feeling pretty brave. He had learned things on that trip. He had been defeated but then slowly pieced things back together. He was confident in not needing to fake anything anymore. He didn't feel the same need to prove himself as he once had.

He was staying at Papa's all of July because his mom, Livy, recommended it. Unlike trips in the past, he wasn't staying with his grandfather because he needed to learn anything specific from the old man or because of Livy's breast cancer treatments. She wanted Wilder down in Texas to look after her dad.

She hadn't seen anything specific, but she knew the clock was ticking on an aging man living in the wilderness away from people. She had noticed his memory on certain things was getting poor. Wilder loved the ranch and maybe he could figure out the best way to help him. He wasn't spying on Papa, but his role had shifted a bit, at least in Livy's mind.

Papa consented to let Wilder handle the roofing job even though it wasn't going to be easy. The next day they went to Amarillo and bought all the supplies and ate at Whataburger. They both had green chile doubles with Dr Pepper. Wilder asked for a lime to go in his Dr Pepper. He told Papa that his mom always did it. Papa was amused. He said that he used to put peanuts in his Dr Pepper, but you needed a bottle for that, of course. Wilder made a mental note to try it.

That evening Wilder unloaded the plywood and shingles and all the other little stuff behind the house and set up a work station. He was used to using his dad's modern equipment and was dismayed with the dust covered tools he rummaged up in the barn. The circular saw was a 60s model with a frayed cord and hadn't been used in a long time. It still cut.

Wilder hadn't been on a horse yet or even looked at the cattle much, but he knew that time was coming.

As he worked the next three days on the roof, he saw Papa making trips back and forth to the barn and then drive to town twice, which was unusual. He figured the cattle drive must be on, even though Papa hadn't mentioned it.

The work was hot, and sweat from Wilder's face dripped on the tar paper and shingles he was working on. He made it a habit, like Papa, to not look at the temperature during the day. He always heard the daily forecasted high as he and Papa sat at the kitchen table and listened to the weather radio every morning, but monitoring the temperature during the day just set you up for wilting. They just worked, whatever had to be done, regardless of what the earth's crust was doing. It helped.

Having finished with the roof, he called home that evening. Wilder had done well, one step at a time, but it was probably the biggest job he had ever done on his own and he wanted to tell his dad. Hank listened and was proud but cautioned Wilder to keep an eye on it during the next big rain. Roof patches were like kitchen sinks, he said, they generally found a way to leak.

Wilder mentioned that he thought he was going on a cattle drive with Papa and Red. Hank nodded on his end of the phone. Hank was no cowboy, but he understood the outdoors and all the risk that came with it. He also understood men, and what it takes to make one. He didn't react over the phone.

Ten minutes after Wilder hung up, the phone rang.

"Wilder, this is mom. Is Papa there?" Her voice was calm and smooth, like always—it was wise. Being in death's shadow for so long had given her an easy gravity that Wilder heard in very few other people. He knew she would be asking about the drive. She had always made him tough, saying she would never raise a wimp, but she also wanted details.

Wilder walked the phone from the kitchen to Papa's chair, making the long cord stretch through the middle of the house.

"Yello," Papa answered.

"Hi Dad," Livy said warmly.

Papa smiled, and laughed. "Am I in trouble?"

"Hardly, I just wanted to say hi and ask about this cattle drive."

"You don't want me to do it?"

"Is it something you have to do?"

"You know the answer to that."

"You just want to do it. You want to do it with Wilder?"

Papa paused. He didn't know the answer to that question. He wasn't used to reflecting on his motivations. He just looked at situations, made his mind up quickly, and then carried out his plans.

Livy knew that too.

"Maybe."

"Well, where are you going to be and how long will it take?"

Papa was back on safe ground.

"Red bought a bunch of pairs off a ranch northeast of Turkey. Sixty-five cows with calves. He has it all worked out to take them right along the river to his place. It's about 20 miles. We'd just be easing them along through fenced ranches all the way ..."

"Like the old days." Livy smiled and finished the line she knew Papa was thinking.

"I guess so, kind of like the old days."

Livy nodded on her end of the phone. She understood. She had done several trips like this when she was young—too young, perhaps. Her dad hadn't lived this long by being careless. They would make it all right. Red was a little bit of a different story.

She had one last question.

"How are you feeling, Dad?"

Between her years-long battle with cancer and his aging, they never knew who was checking on who when they talked anymore, but the question surprised him. His mind immediately went to the doctor's visit he had had yesterday. He hadn't told anyone that his prostate had been on fire lately. The doctor had prescribed a cancer screening ... like he had been doing for years. Maybe Papa would go next month. Somewhere, deep inside, he was worried about sitting on a hard leather saddle for three days.

"Oh, fine. Fit as a fiddle."

Wilder spent the next day going over his gear for the trip. He hadn't been told when they were going but knew he needed to do some significant thinking on it. The first problem was water, which he assumed Papa and Red hadn't considered. The livestock could drink from the muddy Red River, but his backpacking experience told him that wasn't a good idea for people. He hadn't brought his water filter, so he assumed they would be boiling everything.

So he packed a pot and several coffee percolators. He began stacking these on the kitchen table with assorted cans of food. Beans, mostly. He could tell pretty quickly that there was no way these supplies were going to fit on Fancy's back. He went to find Papa.

Papa was working on the 16-foot gooseneck trailer. Wilder watched Papa as he walked from the house to the side of the barn. Papa worked around the rusty red trailer, squirting liberal amounts of WD-40 on all the joints. Wilder could smell the strong oily aroma on the wind.

"Do we have any pack saddles?" Wilder asked. Papa was working the slam-catch on the back gate. He seemed satisfied the third time he slammed the gate and it latched without any assistance. Wilder had just become strong enough to pry open the tough latch, full of rust and wear. Papa had just become unable to open it that way, hence the WD-40 bath.

Papa looked up at Wilder and Wilder looked back at him, unsure if he should repeat himself.

"Pack saddle?" Papa acknowledged the question.

"Don't you think we'll need one for our trip?"

"I suppose so." Papa squirted the trailer latch again. "There's some in the tack room. I haven't used them in years, but you're right, we should have one."

"What horse do you want to pack?"

Papa pondered and set the WD-40 can on the trailer fender. He began to remember why he didn't do this type of thing anymore. Or take trips. Or go anywhere at all, ever, except to town when he had to. Too many decisions. He was tired of decisions.

"Red keeps some donkeys with his yearlings. Maybe we should pack one of them."

Donkey. *What a funny word*, Wilder thought.

He had never been around donkeys but acknowledged, based on books and films, that that they did seem to be pack animals. He didn't see why packing one of their trusted saddle horses wouldn't work. Papa had seven, and most of them rarely got ridden. But he didn't have a strong opinion on the idea either way, so he trudged off to the barn to investigate pack saddles. He found a few, which excited him. He had packed with Gale in the mountains before, but didn't know a lot about it. Two of the panniers that held the gear had mouse nests in them with big holes chewed through the canvas.

Wilder had caught the horses in the grass trap days before so they would be handy if needed. He went out to catch Fancy, his old buckskin mare, to test out the pack saddle. She stood patiently while he rigged up the crossbuck and adjusted the bretching, double cinch, and breast collar. The leather was crusty and dirty, so he spent the next hour working it through with neat's foot oil. The leather came back to life in his hands, like he knew it would.

It was July, but the summer cold front that brought the rain last week seemed to be sticking around. The evenings in West Texas always broke the heat regardless of the daytime temp, and Wilder and Papa usually sat on the porch and read books or just stared at the cottonwoods and big bluestem or whatever the dog was doing. Usually they saw deer work their way down to the creeks from their summer day haunts under cedar trees. That evening, Papa told Wilder they were leaving the next day. Then he motioned for him to follow him. Wilder knew where they were going when they hit the foot path that led to the canyon to the east of the house. Coffee went with them, tongue wagging and triangle ears pointed up.

They walked around a little rise that led into a hackberry grove. The gnarled gray-barked trees stood 30 feet tall, and in a small clearing amongst them stood Grandma's large gray marker inside a short black iron fence. Wilder knew the place but didn't go there much. He didn't know why. He remembered his grandmother. Papa had never brought him there, but they had passed it bringing cattle back and forth to the house pens many times.

Another marker, a white marble cross, also decorated the area. A small lamb lying down was engraved on the stone with the name Josephine True Milam—Papa's sister, stillborn before him a long time ago. All other family members had been buried in town, at the Verbena cemetery. Wilder remembered his grandmother Marian's funeral here, when he was five. A windmill across the fence that kept cattle out of the grove creaked and groaned, pumping up well water. Wilder could just hear the rhythmic splash of the tank being filled from cool springs deep below.

Papa got on his knees and trimmed the grass around Marian's marker. He didn't pull the native grasses up, killing the plants; he grabbed the tops, like a horse, and ripped the stalks and leaves down to ground level. Accustomed to grief now, he was stoic, but not purposefully so.

Marian's marker was for two people. Papa's name—Wendell Irwin Milam—was already engraved next to his wife's. His military branch and WWII were listed under his name. His birthday was there, but then a blank. No death day yet. Wilder had a vague sense that married people did this, but it spooked him to see the gravestone for Papa. It seemed like Papa was on both sides at once. Like he was a ghost, sort of here and sort of gone already.

Wilder mimicked Papa and trimmed the grass around his great aunt's marker. He ran his fingers along the lamb and the deep lettering that spelled her name. It had worn, and in the recesses the stone had turned black with age. Wilder thought about the tiny set of bones under him that never got to see this marvelous ranch. The back of the stone read "The Lord gave, and the Lord hath taken away; blessed be the name of the Lord."

"This is where you'll plant me," Papa unexpectedly said to Wilder.

Wilder didn't know what to say. He could hear the cottonwood trees just down the wash toward the house. They sounded like rushing water in the breeze. He sat down on the buffalo grass that made a cool green mat all around him and leaned back on his palms. He sensed Papa had needed to say that to someone. It made Wilder uncomfortable . . . but also a little proud.

Papa sat down on a black steel bench next to the graves. It had spiderwebs in the corners. Coffee made a circle and sat under the bench with her head up, supervising her people.

"You only plant seeds, I thought," Wilder said, trying to be light about the heaviness that had just descended. He immediately regretted saying it. It was a childish thing to say.

"Did you ever read 'Naked we came into this world, and naked we shall return'?" Papa asked, quoting the book of Job. "I've always thought that was a great line."

"Yes, I have," Wilder replied. "So what do you do in the middle? Before planting."

Papa thought that was a good question for a young man to ask. He wasn't sure of the answer.

"Well . . . try not to be a fool, I guess," Papa mused again at the thought. "Try to keep the code."

Wilder liked the sound of this code idea. "What code?" he asked.

A few long seconds passed as Papa thought.

"I'm not sure exactly. The point is that you have one."

"Well, what's your code?"

"I don't know that I can just say it, like that." Papa opened his hands, at a loss in the line of questioning he had stumbled into. "I suppose I mean that you have to write it yourself. Things you'll do and things you'll not do. A code is your own. A code *has* to be your own. You have to write it because only you can keep it."

Papa looked off toward the trail that led back to the house, signaling that was all he had to say about codes.

"Anything else after that, for this middle ground between your dates?"

Papa smiled. "Maybe honeymoons, three-inch rains, and grandsons," he said. "And cattle drives."

"Yeah, but one of those might kill you."

"That's OK."

"What do you mean that's OK?"

"It's going to be over at some point, son. That's just the way it is. Planted."

Papa had brought up cattle drives, so Wilder decided it was fair game.

"It doesn't have to be this week."

"Maybe not," Papa let out a small chuckle. "That remains to be seen."

"Maybe we should get some trucks. It might be too hard."

"Too hard. I didn't teach you to say too hard. It's foolish maybe . . . but not too hard."

Papa thought for a second. Wilder flicked sand into an antlion's den between his legs. They both were thinking that Papa had just said being a fool was the big problem with life.

"When you run out of usefulness," Papa said, "well, it's time to go. I'm not going to sit in a nursing home and be bottle fed like a calf for the last little bit."

"We'll take care of you."

Papa looked over at him and nodded. "Maybe."

Wilder was kind of angry now. It was partly a cover for his embarrassment at saying something was too hard. But also he knew that families took care of each other. Papa shouldn't question that. This was getting over his head.

"Papa, that's just silly. What would Mom say?"

Papa breathed slowly in and out.

"Wilder, you don't understand. I *want* to die out here. Maybe not today, maybe not for a while still. But this has been my home and if I can work till the end . . . well, that's how I've always seen it.

"Death isn't something I'm afraid of. A bad death, well, that is. I should have died 50 years ago in the war. Everything since then has been gravy. I shouldn't have out-lived my wife. I'd have nothing to complain about if I went today. I don't want to be clawing and grasping for a few more days in the stale air of a hospital.

"I guess it's greedy, but I'd like a good death, out here with my head laying on a round of big bluestem, the wind across my face, and maybe some sweet horse sweat on my hands. The stars take you, and after that I get to see my folks again. And then, Marian.

"And then the ranch will pass to you. Not so bad, huh?"

Wilder's head was spinning. These were ideas he hadn't ever considered. He'd been terrified of his mom's death his whole life. It stalked their family, and his dreams, like a hungry wolf. It was evil to him, all of it.

"Life is a gift, like a butterfly landing on you. But you have to hold it with an open hand."

Papa held his hand out, palm up, as he spoke, then snapped it shut. He stood up and walked away from the little cemetery in the trees.

That night in his room, Wilder wrote out his last Will and Testament.

ʊſ

CHAPTER FOUR

Chicken-fried Steak and Eggs

They met in the kitchen the next day at 6 a.m. Wilder had a pit in his stomach. He and Papa listened to the weather radio while Papa drank coffee, like always. Twenty percent chance of storms tonight, no big deal.

Wilder had loaded all the gear and food into the pickup and felt confident they could live for two days. He had done most of the planning and packing, which surprised him and made him nervous. This seemed like a really big deal, and Papa hadn't talked about it much, other than mentioning dying.

He had made sure Papa had plugged in his cell phone so it would be ready for emergencies. Wilder liked Red and enjoyed his bubbly personality, but the buzzard event had not inspired any confidence in his judgment. Wilder knew long trips revealed all the good and bad in people. Big and Corndog had taught him that.

For the first time in his life, he had the feeling he was taking care of the older people. There was no line, no graduation certificate, but something was happening in the relationship between him and Papa that left him unsettled. He wasn't being looked after, *he* was doing the looking after now.

On the way home from the cemetery the night before, Papa had told Wilder to dig up his "hidey hole" money cache. Wilder had been directed to the spot once before to get some cash for cow work. It was a bit north of the house and marked by a large mesquite knot at the base of a wild plum thicket. The ground was sandy and Wilder uncovered the box easily with his hands. Inside the three-foot steel WWII-era box were bundles of cash and some papers but also an old Colt revolver with a tag that said "Wilder."

Papa said the pistol was Wilder's now. It had been Papa's dad's when he had first homesteaded the ranch. Papa said Wilder was ready for a handgun, and it was a good thing to have in the saddlebags. Wilder replayed the *Lonesome Dove* movie quote in his mind, "Better to have it and not need it, than need and not have it." He hoped he would need it.

Wilder wished it had a leather holster so he could carry it like John Wayne, but instead he packed the unloaded pistol in his saddlebags with a handful of .45 cartridges Papa gave him. In the coming light he caught Fancy and Bud, their two main using horses, and saddled and loaded them in the big gooseneck. Wilder tied dusty rain slickers behind each saddle on top of the saddlebags. Neither piece of gear, saddlebags or slickers, were typically used in West Texas, since it rarely rained and cattle drives were basically extinct.

Wilder and Papa both had their ropes tied on their saddles. Wilder had two. You weren't a cowboy without a rope. A rope meant you were ready to use a horse as a tool, as a partner, and that you were close to cows. Without a rope you were just riding horses.

They left the ranch at 7:30 a.m. to meet Red in Turkey. They passed through Silverton and Quitaque on the way down, and the entrance to Caprock Canyons State Park. A big herd of dark cattle grazed around the gate about a mile from the road, and Papa told Wilder they were buffalo. *Wild cows . . . cool*, Wilder thought. Coffee stood on the center console, watching the road like she always did in the big four-door pickup. Wilder was kind of nervous about Coffee's health but happy to have her along. Being in the wilderness was much better with a dog.

At 9:00 they pulled into the parking lot of the old Turkey Hotel and saw Red's white diesel parked on the side with a horse trailer. There was a horse inside, saddled, and tied along with an unhaltered, bareback donkey in the first compartment. Papa and Wilder both noticed that the front windshield of the truck had been replaced, but the windows were all down and a black streak of dried buzzard smear could still be seen down the middle of the truck. Wilder was right, they must have gotten more than "a buzzard." Papa parked and they went inside the hotel for breakfast with Red.

The old hotel had a string of American flags along its front and two flag poles hoisting the American flag and the Texas flag at equal heights. Wilder knew this was because Texas was the only U.S. state that had been its own country at one time. He had been born in Colorado but was proud to be a fifth generation Texan on his Momma's side.

Red sat at a table with Artemio Leal, his long-time hired hand and cowboy. Art was the big brother of Tequito Leal, or the Little Tick, who Wilder had grown close to when they broke Bluebonnet last summer. Wilder thought about Tequito all the time. He figured Tequito was back in Mexico being the top vaquero for some big, hot ranch. The second rope Wilder had tied onto his saddle was the rawhide-braided reata that Tequito had gifted him. It was a prize possession. The man was "much cowboy," and Wilder wished he was along for whatever they were in for.

Cups of coffee steamed in front of the two men. Red was looking through reading glasses at a map spread out on the table.

"How in the cornbread hell are you?" he said as he looked up at Papa. Papa sat down without answering and Wilder smiled. Wilder stuck out his hand to greet

Red and squeezed the chubby hand hard. Papa skipped Red's hand and shook Artemio's, offering a "buenos dias" and receiving one in return. Wilder did the same.

"Glad you're with us, Wilber." Red looked serious as he comically called Wilder by the wrong name. Getting teased was a sign of respect, and taking it with a smile was a way to earn more respect. A man taking himself too serious could be sniffed out quickly, like a skunk under the house. "We need at least one good man on this outfit. The state police will need someone to explain what happened." Red winked at him.

Papa grabbed the menu and moved it in and out from his face finding focus. Wilder knew he was going to eat big this morning: chicken-fried steak and eggs. He didn't know when he would eat again. And he knew this was going to be the last good meal he would have for a while, so he'd better fuel up before the battle. After they ordered, Red outlined their path for Papa.

"We'll get the cows five miles east of the bridge on Highway 70. The cows are on the Red Mud Ranch. They're cowboy broke. Not a bunch of yearlings or heifers. Older cows that should bump right along until we get to my place. We only need to cross under the bridge by tonight, five miles. We can stay in a bunkhouse trailer that belongs to Justin Wilhoit, my old buddy. Wendell, you know Justin. He spends all his time fishing now."

Papa nodded and said, "But doesn't that put us a pretty good piece from your ranch tomorrow? I was thinking this was just a one night deal."

"Well, it should be, if everything goes right. I don't see why we can't make the last 15 or so miles in one day. But if not, we're prepared to sleep a night under the stars. Like old Charlie Goodnight. I got a couple soogans."

Wilder knew the word "soogan" from his reading. It was an old cowboy word for bedroll.

"I knew Charlie," Papa said, ignoring Red's hopeful plans.

"Here we go again," Red replied.

Papa remained silent. Wilder knew the story, too.

"Wendell, you know Buenos Noches?" Buenos Noches was the well-known nickname for the famous panhandle rancher. Art spoke in their collective Spanglish, which bounced back and forth from English to Spanish, the same dialect Papa and Red used when they talked to him.

"Si, he knew me, you might say," Papa replied, happy to have found a listener.

"Como?" Art asked how, in Spanish.

Papa then relayed the story of the photo Wilder had seen many times. Goodnight had died in 1929, the year after Papa had been born. Papa's dad, Leonidas Milam, had known the Colonel and always stopped to visit him when they passed through Claude, about 20 miles north of the ranch he had established, which Papa still ran, the Tree Water. They had a photo taken on the front porch of the Goodnight house with Papa in a long white baby gown, being held by his dad. Goodnight was old and hunched over in the photo but still had a full head of white hair.

"He was 93," Papa finished, proud of his story.

"He was still a herd bull, too," Red threw in. "Married again at age 91, if I recall."

"He did," Papa confirmed as the assumed expert in all things Goodnight.

The men, Art, Red, and Papa, all seemed to chew on that detail for a bit. Wilder stared at them.

"Well, that's settled then. Wendell, you stay in here

in Turkey and find a wife, and Wilber and I will head the cattle west."

"Isn't Art coming?" Papa asked.

"No bien, Wendell," Art said, "I'm too viejo."

Art wasn't too old, Wilder thought. He couldn't be much past 50, even though he was weathered and creased from an outdoor life. Papa assumed from the answer that Art was busy running the rest of Red's operation, including haying season, it being July.

"Not too old, Art," Papa said, "you're just too smart."

The talk continued as Red laid out the plans for the drive. He had talked to the two ranches they were passing through about gates and what cattle were in those river pastures. The ranch managers had said they were clear of cattle, which was a main reason Red was willing to try the drive. Three men and a donkey mixing cattle would have been a nightmare waiting to happen.

Papa and Red fought over the breakfast tab while Wilder slipped a few extra jelly packets in his pocket. He sopped up all his gravy and egg yolks with three biscuits. Papa left a twenty on the table before getting up to talk to the lady at the front desk of the motel. After a few minutes, Papa joined the others on the front porch.

"Red, we're going to throw our stuff in with you and the donkey. I can leave my rig here for two days. Art, I'll leave the keys in the bed in case you need it for some reason," Papa explained.

"It ain't a donkey. It's a bur-ro." Red rolled his "r"s, pronouncing the Spanish word with flair.

Papa shrugged.

Wilder took that as a cue to unload the horses and start hauling gear to Red's pickup. Wilder grabbed Fancy's lead and loaded her into Red's 32-foot gooseneck, tying her behind Red's big bay horse. Papa followed with Bud. As Wilder was throwing the pack saddle and groceries into the bed of Red's truck, Art came over to him with a sack of something.

"Mijo, take this," Art said with a toothy smile.

"Gracias, Art," Wilder said, then asked, "Que es?" after poking his nose in the cotton sack that weighed about five pounds.

"Cabre . . . goat jerky, from antelopes," Art indicated by making two horns on his head with his finger and thumb in a pistol shape. Wilder was surprised at the gift, and a little frightened. The spices in the bag smelled hot. Real-Mexican-food hot.

"Si, gracias, Art. Mi gusto jerky," Wilder replied.

Art nodded and smiled again.

With nothing else to do in Turkey, they loaded in the pickup for wild country. The truck still smelled like roadkill and buzzard, which was pretty much the same smell. Wilder sat in the back seat with Papa and was pleased the windows stayed rolled down. It looked like Red had done some cleaning of the seats and interior, but the dark stain on the front bench seat was there to stay. Wilder imagined the foul stench that had soaked into the foam cushions.

They drove about ten miles north on Highway 70 to the ranch road that led east to the Red Mud Ranch on the river. The river bottom was similar to Papa's place 40 miles away. The rolling grass-covered foothills bent slowly down to the flood basin of the river. The valley was green and covered in blue-green sand sage and mesquite. After sniffing the seats down and seeming pleased with the aroma, Coffee took up the same position as in Papa's truck.

As it was July, most of the wildflowers were gone, but Wilder still saw patches of red Indian blankets and purple horsemint. It wasn't hot yet, but the humidity from the river and recent rains left a slight stickiness on their skin that the window breeze cooled as they drove. Wilder saw a white and orange antelope buck watching them from a hill.

Occasional cottonwood groves dotted the river bottom, but the dominant sight was the wide open sandy bed of the river. The bare sand was a hundred yards across in many places, with the actual running river only yards across. The red water flowed at a trickle only a few inches deep in some places, in others as deep as four feet.

The problem with all that sand and shallow water was well-known to Papa and Red, not so much to Wilder. Quicksand flourished up and down the muddy drainage from thousands of years of slow trickle. Most of the water flowed underground. Papa had given Wilder one piece of advice concerning river crossings the day before, "Keep an eye on the land. Look for tracks; where the deer and cows cross is where we will, too."

They would be riding for the foreseeable future, or at least the next two or three days. The country looked inhabited. *It isn't so wild*, Wilder thought, *we're close to ranches and roads.*

The truck and trailer and men rumbled and bounced along the washboard caliche road until they passed the sixth cattleguard from the highway, or "hot top" as Papa called asphalt. Red turned onto a two-track pasture road that led north to the river's edge. And then they saw black cattle. Spread out in deep grass with their heads down, Red's herd grazed.

"Welp, there they are," Red said, "the calm before the storm."

Wilder didn't know if the two old men were bracing

and faking it like he was, but he could tell the mood in the truck was a bit more wooden than breakfast had been. Red crawled the pickup out of the two track onto a flat spot and stopped.

The first big problem began when Red tried to unload the burro. The horses had unloaded easily and were tied to the trailer side. Red got a halter on the burro, but he wouldn't budge from his front compartment. The burro was light gray, almost pink, and had a large black cross down his back and across his shoulders. He probably didn't weigh 400 pounds. He was about the size of a mule deer buck.

"Red, has that donkey ever been saddled?" Papa asked, a bit concerned.

"Course not," Red answered from inside the trailer while pulling on the lead rope. "I don't ride donkeys. But I told you it was a burro," Red laughed. "He was wild. I adopted him from the BLM out of Arizona." The BLM was the Bureau of Land Management.

"What makes you think he's going to take a saddle then?"

"Well, maybe the mountain lions in the Grand Canyon saddled him. I don't know. He's gentle, if we can untrack him. Wilber, smack him on the rear."

Wilder grabbed a yucca stalk nearby and went to the front of the trailer from the outside. He whacked the surly burro. He could see it was a jack, meaning he was intact. He whacked the burro as hard as he could, which wasn't very hard since the yucca stalk was brittle and broke. The burro didn't move. Wilder noticed he was staring at Fancy, tied on the outside of the trailer, and Fancy was staring at him. Fancy was the only mare on the trip. He had been around animals enough to know that uncastrated males and mares don't mix well. Fancy had her ears back.

"Mr. Guffey, I think he's scared of Fancy."

Red stopped pulling on the lead and looked at the animals. Wilder threw down his stick and untied Fancy and walked her away from the trailer. The burro untracked and leaped out of the trailer behind Red.

Wilder retied Fancy on the far side of the trailer and came back to help with the supposed saddling of the burro. The animal had a long string of white markings on the left side of its neck. They looked like alien writing.

After Red tied the burro to the trailer, Wilder approached cautiously.

"This burro have a name?" Wilder asked.

"Yes," Red answered, "I just gave him one."

"What is it?"

"Well . . . I can't tell you."

"Oh, it's one of those names . . ." Wilder smiled.

"Yes, it's one of those names."

"He looks like a rabbit. With those ears. Maybe that's why they call jack rabbits, jack rabbits." Wilder thought out loud and tentatively scratched the light, short hair of the animal. The hair was coarse and felt more like fur.

"Call him Rabbit, then. Maybe that will be good luck."

"What's that writing on his neck?"

"That's a freeze brand the government gives burros and mustangs when they are captured. They all have it. It basically says where it was caught and when, and how old it is. The hair comes back white. Kind of cool, huh?"

Wilder petted the brand, running his fingers along the strange markings. He knew about mustangs and their history starting with the conquistadors in the 16th century. That was how the Indians had gotten horses. He had a vague sense that herds of mustangs still roamed free. He knew nothing of burros.

"Captured?"

"Yeah, you can't just walk out into the desert and grab one. These animals are buck wild. They herd them into box canyons with helicopters."

"Why did you buy one?"

"I've had several. The burros just babysit my cattle, calves of course, from coyotes. The mustangs can be broke and ridden. I just love looking at horses, I guess."

Wilder retrieved the pack saddle from the back of the pickup and brought it to Red who was dusting off a saddle blanket and easing it up the burro's back. Papa and Art were watching from a few steps back. The burro didn't seem to mind when Red slid the blanket on. Wilder handed him the pack saddle and stepped back.

Red had been a horse hand all his life and did what he had always done with horses: ask permission, but move forward. For the burro, this meant the saddle was coming, whether or not it was the first time. Red arranged the bretching and double cinch over the back of the saddle and heaved it over the burro's short back.

Nothing happened.

Red turned back to his audience and chuckled, "I told you this jack was broke didn't I?"

Red resumed the saddling, and while he was cautious with the cinching and hooking up the bretching and the breast collar, he moved deliberately, letting the burro know he was in charge and unafraid. With the packsaddle screwed on tight, Red led him away from the trailer.

"His eyes and ears were locked on that mare," Papa offered as a reason for Red's success. Wilder figured this was true as well, which didn't bode well for the trip. Red shrugged.

Wilder held the burro while Papa and Red went through the careful routine of packing the panniers and getting them basically even in weight. Wilder had been taught this by Gale, but had never been in charge of the packing. He was a bit surprised Papa knew about packing as well. To Wilder, this was generally "mountain knowledge" that he had learned from Gale. He got the idea for the first time that there were probably lots of things about Papa he didn't know.

The burro took his load of groceries without a flinch. Red pulled the last strap down and nodded to Wilder, "I need you to drag him."

Wilder was expecting this. He was somewhat disappointed but knew it was his job to shoulder. He had led horses many times and while it restricted the riding so that it was almost impossible to do cow work, someone had to do it. He knew Papa and Red would have their hands full pushing 65 pairs with him riding drag.

Wilder led the burro over to Fancy so he could mount. His lead rope was only a little longer than ten feet, so when Wilder got close to Fancy the burro was obliged to move close to her hind end. He curled up his lip, smelling the mare, and reached out his nose to sniff her more intimately. Fancy was watching.

Lightning quick, she bucked forward, lifting up both rear feet, and punched the burro square in the chest as she let out a furious shriek. The twin hooves thumped the dead weight of the burro like a rifle shot into a sand bag. In the next instant, Fancy returned to standing tied in perfect obedience. Wilder's eyes bugged out. He hadn't thought Fancy had a mean bone in her body.

The blow knocked the burro over backwards. He

then flopped to his side crushing the pack saddle. He didn't get back up. Papa, Red, and Art rushed over. Coffee started barking at the limp animal on the ground.

"We ain't even left yet and already we got a man down," Red grumbled as he took in the scene.

"Ay-yih-yih . . . esta muerto?" Art wondered aloud if the burro was dead.

The burro lay there on his side, breathing hoarsely. He looked pretty uncomfortable with the packsaddle bowing him out and up in the middle. Papa picked up the lead and slapped him on the rump with the end of it.

"You ain't dead yet," he said.

Papa pulled the burro's head to the side, and he raised up some. Another tug got his front two feet under him and then his hind legs. With a final pull Papa had him upright again.

"I guess you'll think twice about nosing up on strange women," Papa rebuked the animal. He patted his chest looking for tears. No blood.

"Good advice," Red said patting his belly. "I could have used it when I was young and handsome."

Wilder left Fancy tied and stepped up to hold the burro's lead rope. The burro just stared back at him with dark eyes that never seemed to change. Wilder was used to reading a horse's mood by its eyes. A horse could be experiencing a range of emotions, from content to enraged, and their eyes and how much white they were showing always displayed their mood. But the burro just looked bored. It stared back at Wilder, stone-faced. The animal was a blank slate.

Papa and Red were surveying the damage on the pack saddle and panniers. Neither man felt like unpacking everything. If something was broke they would find it in camp tonight. The old saddle had held together, presumably because burros don't weigh much compared to a horse. They were ready to get going.

"OK, good enough," Red declared. "You boys ready to push cattle?"

They nodded, somewhat more relaxed than before. The action, the violence, perhaps, had put them in the game. It was like a first punch that bleeds off all the fear and anxiety that comes before danger. They were ready now to ride off and see what would happen next.

CHAPTER FIVE

Boys with Cows

Wilder waved goodbye to Art and the pickup and trailer and air conditioning. Papa and Red were already easing toward the river to scoop up the herd. Rabbit looked sullen at the end of his lead rope. Wilder pulled him with one arm and handled Fancy's reins with the other. He could already tell this was going to be a tough job. He dallied the lead on his saddle horn to get Rabbit moving and tickled Fancy with his spurs to let her know she now had to pull the beast that she had just kicked away.

"I know, girl, it doesn't make any sense," he said out loud.

Rabbit gave in to the mare's pull, and Fancy switched her tail as if to remind him of his manners. Rabbit walked to the right, keeping clear of her potent hooves.

Like Wilder, Papa and Red wore leather leggings called "chinks," which were cut off just below the knee to provide leg protection but also airflow. Papa rode Bud, a sorrel gelding—a red horse with a matching mane and tail. Red was riding a huge bay gelding he called Burrito. Wilder had asked Red one time why he named him Burrito. Red said he bought him at an auction, taking a chance, and the young rodeo gal riding him had warned him that the gelding was a lot of horse. Red had sassed her good-naturedly about his cowboy skills, and she had said back, "I'm just saying, for this horse maybe you should eat a few less burritos."

Red's belly stuck out and bounced up against the saddle horn when he was in any gait except a slow walk. Red was fat, but fat in an athletic way. His bottom was skinny and he had a spring to his step like an NFL lineman that weighed 300 pounds. Wilder noticed with interest that Red had a leather scabbard tied to his saddle that held what looked to be a very short rifle. He figured it was probably a .22.

Both old men rode with their backs straight, which was a balance Wilder was still perfecting. He still tended to lean forward and slouch at times. Real horseman never had to cheat like that. A good horseman was like a rooster crowing on a fence in the dark. And while slower on foot than they used to be, Papa and Red still rode like young men. They didn't have to speak or gesture or get past a trot but occasionally. They read cattle and landscape like a newspaper, making all the small movements and adjustments that kept a herd of over a hundred animals moving in the right direction.

Papa and Red had disappeared as Wilder rode to the east end of the herd, staying far back. He assumed they were scouting the river bottom and foothills to make sure they had all of them. They couldn't get a hard count with the cows all spread out. They would leave with whatever cows they found in the immediate area.

The herd was on their side of the river and Papa and Red had discussed leaving them in that position all the way, if possible. Crossing the sandy flood plain was to be avoided unless absolutely necessary. Red reappeared from checking the opposite bank and eased between the cows and the river without pressuring them. He waited for Wilder to lead Rabbit up to the rear drag position, and Papa waited in the foothills after his quick search. No strays had been brought in.

There wasn't anything else to do, Wilder figured, so, taking cues from the old men who were now pointing west on their horses and standing, he kicked up Fancy to a walk. When Wilder started talking to them, the cows closest to him raised their heads and stared back. They were gentle-looking older cows with goofy calves spotting the grassland around them. Several calves were already bedded after the morning feed.

"Whooooo cows . . . whooo," was his call, practiced and refined over his few years horseback. It was gentle and personal. He was talking to the cows. Some cowboys whistled, some let out short "yips" and "heys," but the gentle "whooo cows" worked for Wilder. He popped his rein ends on his chinks, leather on leather, as the attention getter.

More cows lifted their heads as he applied pressure by moving his horse closer. This was always the tense moment on a gather. Who was going to win the battle of wills? The cows were happy where they were, and while the cows didn't know it, three horsemen could never control a mob of strong, heavy animals in open country. Ranching was kind of absurd in that sense: That a man could endeavor to control thousands of acres of raw land and then fill it with dangerous and untamed animals. Sometimes it worked. It usually worked, in fact. But there was always the chance—the eventuality—that weather, fire, or the unpredictable nature of livestock could and would turn on you. It was about as far from a desk job as one could get.

Without horses, ranching would not work. Wilder was always amazed how much rough ground he could cover when mounted. Now Fancy was carrying him and a saddle, and pulling a reluctant 400-pound burro, and she could do it all day. Wilder's skinny body would be sapped out in minutes of similar work.

A horse was like some kind of superhero power suit. It magnified a man's body; lungs bigger, legs longer, muscles stronger, speed and endurance quadrupled. A mounted man became a super human of sorts. It was no wonder the Aztecs called the conquistadores "gods" when they first saw them riding horses in the 16th century.

But gentle cows and good cowboys helped the odds in ranching, and these cows had been through this drill many times. Slowly they responded to Wilder's pressure, bunched up, and saw Red to the right and Papa to the left. A lead cow wheeled and headed west with her calf. Soon every hoof was up and moving in the right direction. Calves darted this way and that but could be largely ignored. They would follow their mothers with the heavy bags of milk swaying back and forth between their hind legs.

There were no bulls. They had already been pulled off after breeding the cows earlier in the summer. Most of the calves were big, 300 pounds being the smallest. A hundred and thirty animals, times four, made over 500 hooves. Wilder could hear the grass swish back and forth as they lumbered through the river valley. It was a great sound. Rain had been plentiful this year.

This is going to be easy, Wilder thought.

Which was a thought he would recall many times over the next few days . . .

Wilder let Fancy lead the way, and she established a gait that made Rabbit trot forward every four or five steps. He stopped pulling back on the lead Wilder had dallied to his saddle horn. The cows strung out a bit and generally behaved themselves. They weren't on an established trail but the foothills were covered in shinery oak and sage and didn't provide any serious reasons for a derailment.

A wind from the south picked up and Wilder readjusted his gray felt hat. It had a good sweat seal now. Only greenhorns lost their hats when riding.

After an hour plodding along, Wilder saw the first five-wire fence line that would stop their progress. Red said there would be several of these and that no other cow herds awaited to cause problems. Still, a fence line meant Papa or Red would have to ride ahead and open the gate without any cattle running back the way they came. Then he would have to retake his flank position and push them through a 20-foot opening the cows had likely never used before.

Papa rode toward the gate, probably feeling that the cows would be less likely to run uphill than toward the river, as they could have if Red had moved to the front. Wilder decided he would do his best to hold them, if needed, and would drop Rabbit's lead if absolutely necessary to turn the herd in case they took off. Rabbit wouldn't have a home ranch to run to and would probably stay put or follow Wilder anyway.

Before Papa reached the gate, Wilder heard a loud motorized sound. It sounded like a motorcycle on the highway. They were far from the highway, and the noise broke the stillness of the valley. The sound was getting closer. Wilder saw Papa stop at the gate and turn his horse around.

Then Wilder saw dust. Two men on four wheelers appeared in the foothills behind the herd and were roaring toward them. They rode big green and black quads with knobby tires. They raced along the valley floor, occasionally hitting the sandy bottom of the floodplain and throwing rooster tails of mud behind them. The cows turned around to face the intruders. Wilder held steady.

It seemed like the men were going to race right into the herd, which would undoubtedly scatter them hopelessly. Red turned his horse and trotted back down the river to meet the four wheelers.

The machines motored down and stopped when Red got close to them. Red wasn't yelling at the men, so it seemed like a friendly meeting. Wilder wanted to ride over and see what the deal was. The men looked to be in their twenties, and wore jeans and t-shirts and backwards baseball caps. There was a rifle mounted in a plastic scabbard on one of the machines. Red talked with the men for several minutes, then he turned and took back up his position. The men started their machines and peeled out toward the east, leaving dust and mud in their wake and taking their obtrusive mufflers with them.

Red stopped his horse, which seemed to signal "back to work" for Papa and Wilder. The cows just stared in the direction the machines had taken.

Papa moved to the front of the herd and rode the fence line at a walk to the wire gate about 100 yards from the river. Cows usually have one good run in them on a gather, but these hadn't acted spooky one bit. Now they simply looked around in all directions, taking cues from the cowboys' positions about what they were supposed to do next. Papa had the gate open and was quickly remounted and trotting back to his position. The three cowboys began to squeeze the herd toward the gate.

A cow and two calves turned back on Wilder and he spurred Fancy to the right to head her off. His saddle creaked as the lead rope pulled on the horn and snapped Rabbit into attention. The two large movements of horse and burro quickly scared the cow back into the herd that was now along the fence and looking for a way through, but the two calves squirted by. Wilder reined Fancy around to chase them but caught

57

Papa in his eye as he did. He was facing the fence and seemed to be deliberately not looking Wilder's way. Wilder figured Papa had surely seen the escapee calves and was cueing him to ignore them. So he reined Fancy up and turned back toward the herd.

The cows were going through now. Simple. Once one went, they would all pour through in time. Slowly they moved up and pushed them through. Soon all three riders were at the gate together. Neither Papa nor Red made a move toward the calves behind them.

Wilder spoke up, "You want me to get those calves?"

"What do you think?" Papa offered. Red got down to get the gate. It was Wilder's job to get the gate, being the youngest man, but he had stayed saddled knowing the calves had to be brought up first.

Wilder was puzzled. Papa obviously knew something he didn't.

"Look at those calves now," Papa added.

Wilder turned. They were 50 yards back with their noses in the wind toward the herd. Wilder understood.

"We just have to get out of the way, right?"

"Right," Papa said, and added, "You can always trust a calf to do two things. To always do the stupid thing. And always find their momma."

Wilder nodded and began moving Fancy along the fence out of the way of the gate. Papa rode next to him.

"Good job on the cow. Remember, we're herding cows, not calves. Get the cows and the calves will follow. Not to mention, there's a fence around this whole place. The cows really can't go anywhere. It ain't the wild old days when they could run all the way to Mexico."

The calves ran through a minute later and bawled back and forth with their mothers before rushing in for a greedy milk suckle. All the other cow/calf pairs were doing the same thing, feeling a lack of pressure from the horsemen. Red waited for Wilder and Papa at the gate. Red set the gate behind them, and Papa and Wilder dismounted and stood next to Red. They all readjusted and tightened their cinches.

Papa grimaced when he swung down. His prostate gland was aching and it made his whole trunk hurt. He couldn't imagine not finishing this little chore, but riding the hard leather seat was starting to feel like torture.

Red took off his hat and wiped his forehead with his shirtsleeve. They were all dripping but all wore long-sleeved shirts. Red, being light-skinned, knew more acutely than the rest that the sun was trying to kill you. All outdoorsmen knew this and stayed covered regardless of the temperature. Only city people wore shorts and t-shirts outside.

"That went pretty slick," Red said, "We do that about five more times and we're home." Wilder slurped from one of the two Nalgene bottles he had stowed in his saddle bags. Then he tentatively fingered a piece of Art's jerky. He didn't need much. His chicken-fried steak and eggs and hash browns were doing their job.

"Wind from the south, kills the drouth," Papa said.

"Yeah, it's going to storm somewhere on the dryline tonight," Red added. The air was feeling more humid by the minute.

Papa and Red were both thinking the same thing. Rain was always welcome. Always. That was gospel. There was no gospel like rain in ranch country, except maybe the real gospel. But rain was a pretty close second, if not almost the same thing, when you got right down to it. God, church, and rain were all wrapped up into a similar bundle.

But a crackling summer storm exposed on horseback didn't sound like fun for anyone.

Papa and Red joined Wilder in grabbing a quick lunch. They drank from their canteens and pulled out assorted granola bars and dried summer sausage and crackers. Papa methodically peeled an orange. Its bright sticky scent stood out against the sage and humidity.

Wilder was still wondering about the four-wheelers. "What did those guys want?" he asked.

"They were a few of Wiley's hands. Asked if we needed any help," Red answered.

"What were they going to do on quads?"

"Same thing we're doing."

"But they didn't have horses," Wilder said, confused.

"There's not a horse on the 50,000 acres of the Red Mud. Wiley, the manager, got rid of them. As well as ropes and cowboys."

"How do they work cows then?"

"Wilber, I guess you ain't been around much. There aren't many ranches left like your grandaddy's. Cowboys and horses are too big of a liability for some of the big places. Small ones, too. They work everything in a chute and feed gas to their ponies."

Wilder hadn't ever heard of this.

"Not to mention there just aren't that many men who can do the work. It doesn't pay anything, and it takes a lifetime to learn. Wendell ought to name his place the Tree Water Museum." Red laughed.

Wilder was incensed, but he figured he should shut up. He had been in awe of the Red Mud Ranch seeing it spread out on the river, imagining the years of cowboys and horses and traditions that it represented. Now it seemed diminished. Less.

"Figure we got five miles to the bridge and the bunkhouse . . ." Papa asked, breaking up the question and answer session. The pain in Papa's seat was making him think ahead, which annoyed him. Red didn't answer. Papa knew where they were.

Wilder took the cue and turned from the conversation to fish some apples out from the pack saddle panniers. He offered them to Papa and Red. They each ate one and gave the cores to their horses who paused a second from speed grazing the buffalo grass at their feet. They greedily nosed the cores and crunched down the sweet apple.

Red looked at Wilder. "Wilber, you like that jerky?"

Wilder was chawing on a piece now. It was good, and not as hot as he had feared, although he liked hot.

"Yawp," he muttered back while chewing the leather in his mouth.

"He tell you what he makes it out of?"

Wilder swallowed, "Yes, cabre. Antelope."

"Yes, that's good. But you know it ain't antelope season, right?" Red snickered and swung up on his horse with a big suck in of air, followed by an exhale when he was seated.

Wilder looked at him funny. *So what if it wasn't antelope season*, Wilder thought. *He could have shot it back in November.*

"I just figured you would have learned to leave the roadkill to the buzzards." Red chuckled out loud and kicked Burrito into a trot toward the river.

ᘐᘜ

CHAPTER SIX

Close to God

Coffee limped a little as they spread out around the backside of the cattle and began their push. She stayed with Papa. Papa sat gingerly at first when he remounted and then worked back into the semi-twisted position that was tolerable.

The sky had clouded up to the west, the direction they were going, and the small explosions of clouds began rising and billowing. They rose and rose, and the riders watched, knowing an anvil cloud was coming next. Soft rainstorms didn't happen in the hot summer months in the panhandle.

The cows behaved, and even though they were in new country, they had figured out the drill. A cow with a swollen bag had taken the lead and nosed her way through the river bottom like the head of a snake dragging its body along.

Wilder catalogued the wildlife. Every motte of soapberry and hackberry trees held deer or turkeys. The whitetails wore their thin red summer coats and trotted reluctantly away from their shade as the cows pushed through. Mule deer were more likely to stare at the cows and men with their big mule ears pointing up like jack rabbits. They didn't look too different from Rabbit. Scissortail flycatchers worked the river insects, doing midair battle with dragonflies. Wild turkeys stomped off through the big bluestem after being roused. They looked like the packs of velociraptors in the *Jurassic Park* movies, Wilder thought.

Buzzards soared over them and Wilder felt nauseous in the hot air.

The day drifted into the afternoon and the anvil

cloud loomed before them. They pushed the cows off the river and into the foothills to give them a drink at a windmill tank. When the cows had their fill, the riders met at the tank to let their horses drink. Three horses and one burro dipped their noses in and sucked deep and fast. It was a good sound, maybe one of the best sounds—a thirsty horse drinking. A beautiful sound that few people knew. Wilder knew there was a poem in there somewhere. He made a mental note, maybe tonight he would try and find words for it.

"What do you think about that cloud, Wendell?" Red asked, worry in his voice. There weren't any heroes around lightning strikes. Lightning was an equalizer when it came to bravery.

"Nothing we can do but hope it misses us," Papa replied.

"You ever been hit by lightning?"

Papa chuckled, "No, you?" he asked back looking at Red in amusement.

"No. They're one per customer, though. Whitey Rector was hit. Turned every hair on his body white. He lived another 30 years. Did you know him?"

"I knew his kids. They said he wasn't scared of nothing after that. He was a welder in the oilfield. I always figured lightning would have the opposite effect. But it made him feel an immunity to death."

"Or real close to God," Red countered.

"Yeah, real close."

Wilder listened to Fancy slurp and play in the clear tank water. He got down and refilled everyone's canteens and his bottles from the windmill pipe that was pumping fast with the south wind sailing through the blades above them. The mill was moving too fast; it gave him the chills. His bottle beaded up with condensation from the cool water seeing daylight for the first time in thousands of years. It tasted much better than the stale water he had been drinking, if a bit salty.

"Well, we only got a short way to the bridge, about a mile after that bend," Red explained. "We push them under the bridge and there's a gate on the other side. After that they can scatter. The bunk house is just up the foothills to the north about a hundred yards."

That was about an hour's worth of work, Wilder thought. But he didn't think they had that much time before the storm rolled through. They could already see the yellow glow from lightning filling the cloud like a lightbulb.

"We're in a hurry," Red said, "better slow down."

Wilder swung up and knew Red's little joke was true. Papa had taught him this cow wisdom since he was old enough to ride in the pickup and drive on his lap, when he was about five. The only way to move cows fast, was slow. If you pushed the shaky alliance between cowboys and cows too much, mayhem erupted. Cows were dumb in some ways and could be loosely controlled in open country, but they had their limits and, when asked to do too much too fast, could scatter like quail and leave fences smashed in their wake.

They started hearing thunder, and Wilder began counting seconds off between the light flashes and the noise. It was about five seconds per mile, Wilder had been told. One thousand one . . . one thousand two . . . one thousand three . . . Seven miles away they boomed. Then three. The sky darkened and it appeared twilight instead of five o'clock.

Wilder watched Papa to see if he was going to pull out his rain slicker. It was still tied behind his saddle. Getting wet wasn't a big deal, he figured. It was probably 95 degrees, although in the strong wind and shade from the cloud it didn't feel that hot.

Then a big bolt hit on the caprock a couple miles to the south, over Papa's head. It shook the valley and the horses and cows all stopped to look. Fancy's ears stood up and her mane whipped in the cooling air. The rain was coming. Papa rode to Wilder. Wilder waited.

More thunder boomed, and lightning began flashing in every direction. The blurry blue rain appeared in front of them. Papa kicked Bud up to a lope as Wilder waited, fumbling behind him with his yellow, mouse-eaten slicker. He pulled it out, which spooked Rabbit a bit. Fancy didn't mind.

Papa pulled up and swung down fast. "Wilder, get down," he ordered.

Wilder did so, holding both Fancy's reins and the burro lead rope.

"We got to get as low as we can, son," Papa said, looking nervous. "Tie those horses to a mesquite and come on."

Wilder had never been through this before. There was a six-foot wiry mesquite handy, and he tied Fancy's reins in a slip knot as best he could. Generally, you never tied a horse hard with leather reins, especially not in open country, but it was the best he could do. Wilder glanced up and the wall of white rain was a hundred yards in front of him. He was completely exposed.

Then the rain hit and staggered the boy. It roared and the wind delivered the cold drops sideways.

Wilder found his balance and followed Papa downhill toward the river at a fast trot. Bud was tied ten feet away from Fancy. The burro balked and wouldn't lead without Herculean pulls from Wilder, side to side, like tacking a sail boat. Papa turned around and hollered back at him as loud as he could, "Leave the burro!"

Wilder dropped the lead and ran to catch Papa who

was walking fast, carrying his slicker and trying to get it on through the wind and rain. It fluttered at his side like a flag. Water soaked Wilder's shirt and it clung to his thin frame.

Fifty yards from the river they came to a small wash that made a bowl about 20 yards across and ten feet deep as it drained down to the river. Papa yelled and told Wilder to squat down and sit on his feet. Soaking wet and perplexed, Wilder did so. Papa walked 30 feet away and did the same thing. Water streamed down the front brims of their hats. They pulled their slickers over their necks and over the backs of their hats. Red was nowhere to be seen.

Wilder turned his back to the storm and remembered his night on the Spanish Peaks a month before. The storm had been awful then but was worse now, although he was thankful there was no hail. Papa hunkered and stared at Wilder, looking sick. Coffee had stayed with him, squished in between his legs, which steadied both of them in the onslaught.

Wilder caught some movement to the right, about 50 yards out. He saw Rabbit breaking for the river bottom and a small forest of three or four cottonwoods. The lead rope was dragging behind him and he ran to the side, having figured out how to move without stepping on it. *Smart burro*, Wilder thought. Horses never seemed to figure that out.

Then the world turned bright white in one big flash. Momentarily deaf and partially blind, Wilder saw Rabbit fall over like a domino.

And he felt close to God.

ᏌᏇ

CHAPTER SEVEN
Baptized Again

It seemed to Wilder that there was always a point that screamed—*time to give up*. Whether it was getting hammered by 40 points in a basketball game, or when math homework just did not make any sense, or when his little sister Molly would not stay out of his room.

He felt that point was made very clear when the lightning bolt hit the tallest of the cottonwoods Rabbit was trotting toward. It exploded the tree and left a trail of smoke and flames in the downpour. One main branch came crashing down and it looked like a hawk nest had caught fire.

The ground felt like an earthquake and Wilder screamed at the surprise and violence of the flash. All his normal sensations had been suspended by the power of the bolt. The world seemed to be floating, everything changed in an instant. He had never felt so vulnerable. Seeing lightning close by from a building or a car was one thing, but this felt like walking with lions on the African savannah, or swimming with sharks.

The ground around the tree was smoking and so was Rabbit. Wilder looked at Papa and when he eventually looked back at Wilder he held his hand out to motion him to stay put. Rabbit didn't move.

Then it looked like he did. Maybe it was just the wind, but the burro's head seemed to strain up. He was bowed up in the middle like he had been before because of the pack saddle's bulk under his side.

Wilder felt close to God with death so near, but also a little angry at him. It wasn't really a good closeness. How could he just zap people like that? Wilder understood it wasn't as simple as that, that God wasn't maliciously enjoying killing people in little puffs, but it seemed arbitrary and, well, cold.

He thought of God as a protective father, not as a loose cannon that left live wires lying around the house for two-year-olds to find. Would God zap him, too? If the weather front and meteorological science happened to like the square foot in the little wash on the Red River where he now shivered? A hundred pounds of 13-year-old boy ready to be cooked alive? He hadn't even shaved yet.

Well, meaningfully shaved.

The rain poured and the storm front moved east as he pondered the cosmos. The thunder rumbled and Wilder imagined that he'd be able to feel the lightning coming and jump over a few feet. His boots felt squishy.

After 15 minutes the rain lessened to a straight down shower, the kind they craved in ranch country, and Papa walked over to him. Rabbit hadn't moved any more.

"Wilder, I'm sorry about this," Papa said, as he gave the boy a full-on hug. Wilder pulled back at first, not sure what was happening as the old man opened his arms to him. But he figured it out and gave in. He hugged him back. He smelled like wet horses. Which was about as good a smell as you can have.

"Did you think we were going to die?" Wilder said when they separated.

"I thought about it. I sure did. I'm sorry I had you out here."

"It wasn't your fault. How can we tell what God is going to do?"

Papa paused on that one. Wilder blamed God. Papa blamed himself.

"God gave us brains to stay out of storms, I guess.

Maybe something is wrong with my brain." Papa looked over toward the burro. "He didn't give Rabbit the same brains."

"You think he's dead?"

"Probably."

They trudged through the wet grass in soaked high-heeled riding boots toward the black, wet mass that used to be a burro. The cottonwood trunk still smoldering. When they approached to within ten feet, the way they would if they were coming up on a downed deer, Rabbit's head swung over and looked at them. Wilder's heart leaped.

He ran over and slid down next to him and patted his side. Rabbit looked him in the eyes. It seemed like a human to human look. Wilder told him he was a good burro and patted him soft and easy. Wilder looked at his hooves expecting them to be melted off. He had read about that in a book.

Papa grabbed the lead and Wilder got back out of the way. Papa tugged on the burro's head, trying to get him up. He knew that generally a downed horse was a dead horse, but if you could get them on their feet they might make it. Wilder tugged the pannier loops off the packsaddle, unloading 100 pounds of unnecessary weight in the two large canvas bags. Papa pulled and Wilder pushed and encouraged Rabbit. With a grunt the burro got his front feet into the mud, sat there for a bit, and, with Wilder's help, planted all four shaky legs.

Red gave a loud holler from behind them. He was riding Burrito and shaking his head.

"I've never seen such a thing . . . my oh my. Wow!" He kept muttering as he trotted up and swung down. He patted Rabbit all over and checked his hooves and legs. He even lifted up the Rabbit's front lip and looked in his mouth.

"I would not believe it if I hadn't seen it, Wendell. You ever seen an animal get electrocuted before?"

"No, never have. But this burro took a full dose."

"Did you guys see it?"

"Yep, we weren't but a baseball toss away from here. I thought maybe we were all dead," Papa mused. "I haven't been so scared since, since . . . well, you know when."

Red looked Papa in the eye. He knew Papa was being serious. He knew when. But he figured Papa wasn't scared for himself this time.

"Yeah, well, I'm glad we came through all right. I guess this burro still wants to work."

They stood around another ten minutes on what seemed like holy ground now, ignoring the cattle, and talked through the bolt, the rain, the exhilaration that comes from realizing you are alive after a battle. Soft rain pelted their hats and slickers in little pitter pats that were no longer threatening. They were warm again, the breath of life after a painful delivery.

Finally they decided they had a job to finish, regardless of near death experiences. Wilder and Papa led Rabbit back to their horses. Wilder made sure he had re-attached the panniers to the packsaddle properly. Fancy and Bud had their rumps turned to the storm and seemed no worse for wear. What had been a life-changing, near religious, event for the men was merely another day in the outdoor life of a ranch horse. There were no blankets or barns to run to. There never had been.

Wilder swept the water off his seat and swung up. He figured he was pretty cowboy now. He was soaked head to toe, baptized again on the Red River.

The cows were grazing in the wet grass like petting zoo sheep. The men gathered them back up and soon could see the road and watch the occasional semi roaring down it with a trail of rain mist rooster-tailing behind. The bridge was plenty long and offered a much wider gate than their previous crossing, but it was still a bottleneck that would force the cows through an unusual opening and into the sandy river floodplain.

Wilder could tell that Red didn't want to cross the river if he didn't have to and was keeping the cows away from it. Papa squeezed the herd now, too, hoping to line them out and drive them under the bridge on firm soil. The quicksand warning was in the back of Wilder's mind. Rabbit stumbled a bit but seemed to be keeping up. If the cows turned back, Wilder figured he could drop the lead and the burro would stay put and might even help block the cows from looping around.

The cows got snuffy about the bridge. A colony of barn swallows lived under it and the small black and tan birds had come out after the fresh rain and were swirling around the bridge and swooping into the river bank for insects and fresh mud to add to their cliff dwellings that lined the large I-beams underneath the structure. The lead cow balked, and the rest of the herd took her cue.

A car raced down the road and honked several times. Cowboys were a common sight in the panhandle, but Wilder figured maybe some out-of-towners got a kick out of seeing the anachronism they represented. These cows had probably never had anything but trees over their heads, and so the looming cavern of the bridge, along with the swarming bird and car traffic, gave them second thoughts.

Red took a chance and decided to lead them by riding point. Sometimes cows would follow a lead horse. Larger gathers and drives always had a man out front. Red eased his horse under the bridge, taking care to never point the horse toward the cows. They eyed him with suspicion. Wilder slid over closer to the river and Papa came his way about 30 yards.

Coffee had been trailing them, not doing much, but now sensed the urgency. She got between Wilder and Papa and laid her ears back and growled a few times. She knew not to bark but made her presence known to the cows.

Wilder called to the cows, "Whooo . . . cows, come on babies . . . whooo!" and popped his reins. Papa made his "Yip, yip" call. Wilder figured it was a coyote mimicry, which was pretty smart.

Red moved under the bridge to the right of the river plain, taking a step every couple seconds. Wilder and Papa pushed, hoping their little teakettle of cattle wouldn't tip over.

Surprisingly, a couple of swirling calves glanced at the dark figure of Red under the bridge and took him for a cow. They broke toward Red and bawled. Their mothers responded, and soon the herd had been convinced that the bridge was the way to go. Papa and Wilder came up quickly and closed the gap between them and the bridge. Some of the cows slipped as they rushed through. Wilder soon found out why: silt had pooled and eddied under the bridge for 50 years and was slick as watermelon seeds. The red clay made sucking sounds on Fancy's hooves as she picked her way under the bridge. He agreed with the cows, the under-bridge crossing was spooky.

It was a great place for trolls, or for rattlesnakes to lie cooling in the heat of the day, and he looked for them but didn't see any. Wilder and Papa smiled at each other as they rode close together now, a big relief melting off both of them. They just had to push the herd through the fence gate on the other side, which

Red was now opening, and they could rest their wet bones and minds until tomorrow.

Red tried his luck—or perhaps his finely tuned cow sense—again and kept the point to the gate. The cows never broke their trot; they ran right through. Wilder could see the bunkhouse on the other side of the river, half a mile to the north.

"Slicker than snot," Red said as he watched the cattle fan out and look back at the cowboys. Wilder swung down to man the gate. He handed his reins to Papa with Rabbit's lead tied to his saddle horn. He struggled with the taut wire gate but got it closed by pulling with two hands on the gate post and holding the wire gate against his chest. Rusty barbs scratched his thin chest through his shirt and made his skin bleed a bit, but he didn't mention it.

They were all eager to hit the house, even if no one was willing to say it. Red picked a river crossing by letting Burrito have his head and probe with his feet. He leaned in close to the water and sniffed at it before putting a foot down. The water was up some but still only inches in the shallows and about two feet in the current along the far bank. They splashed through on hard sand and walked quietly in the light rain up the foothills to the trailer house.

It didn't look like much, but none of them were expecting much. Weeds and grass were grown all around, and the driveway looked like it hadn't been used in a long time. The trailer had to be 50 years old, with faded turquoise striping on the bottom of its aluminum shell. A single-wide with a small, sagging, covered porch on the front that didn't scream welcome. An outhouse was huddled into a shinery oak grove 30 yards behind it. It was a cowboy place.

It was a ranch bunkhouse, or had been at one time,

so there was a wire pen in the back for the horses, about two acres of grass, and a dirt tank formed by a dam between two hills.

Wilder knew it was full of mice when he saw the diamondback rattlesnake slithering along where the front porch met the trailer. *Welcome home*, he thought.

〰️

CHAPTER EIGHT
Snake House

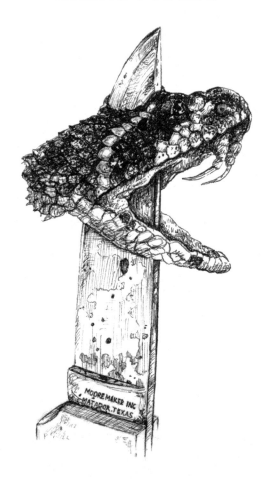

Papa didn't offer a "be careful" as Wilder swung off his horse to dispatch the snake. He knew Wilder had killed many snakes on his own. Papa rarely killed them anymore. Snakes had their way, as he had his. He knew their way and left them to it. But it took a long time to know a snake's way.

The boy handed his reins to Papa and slipped off his belt, removing his Mooremaker sheath and knife and sliding them into his back pocket. There was a half-alive elm tree near the house, and Wilder retrieved a three foot dead branch from it. Papa and Red sat horseback to watch the young protégé.

Wilder approached the snake with the stick. It reluctantly coiled up and raised its head. It buzzed and then struck a few times at the stick, going from content to hopping mad in seconds, which raised Wilder's heartbeat. No matter how many snakes you killed, they still got your attention. Pain and even death awaited if you got careless. A rattlesnake was a liquid violence, a cup that if tipped over would spill in the same direction every time. Which also made them predictable and, in some ways, easy to kill. Wilder slipped the stick under the snake and flipped him off the porch a good ways. The snake flew like a baton, end over end, and landed in the wet grass.

Coffee noticed the action and came up quickly and barked at the snake from several feet away. She knew snakes better than all the men. She had a snake bark, Papa would say. She knew to stay back and that her people were already alerted. Wilder stomped carefully to the grass where the snake was now slithering away.

He whacked it with the brass belt buckle on the end of his leather belt. The snake stopped and didn't coil. Wilder whacked it two more times, hard.

Then he dropped his belt and pulled out his knife from his back pocket. He studied the writhing and paralyzed snake like a coyote and then pounced with his leather boot to secure the head. Head under heel, he severed the head with his knife. Then he stabbed the triangle shaped head, gaping wide with both upper fangs gleaming white, and held it up for Papa and Red to see.

"That your first time to do that, Wilber?" Red teased.

"Yes," Wilder sassed back, feeling his oats, "usually I just grin 'em down."

"Oh," Red laughed, "is that right, like old Davy Crockett."

"Yeah, like him."

Wilder threw the snake body up on the porch where it slithered in "S" shapes back and forth and smeared blood all over the warped wood floor from its head stump. Coffee ran up to it and took it in her mouth and shook it back and forth violently. Papa laughed.

Wilder buried the head deep in the damp sandy soil using the stick to dig with. He knew Coffee would stay away, but it was still a routine he followed like law. His dad had failed to listen to Papa's warning about cutting off snake heads when he had first come to the ranch before Wilder was born. Hank's beaten down rattler had spent the night in the back of his truck, where he had thrown it thinking it was plenty dead. In the morning it was fully alive and striking when Hank checked on it. It was a family story that Hank never lived down.

The snake killing over, they assembled at the small uncovered back porch where an assembly of steel saddle racks and a hitching post slowly crumbled back into the earth. It was with great joy that they finally dismounted for the day and slopped their soaked saddle blankets and saddles on the racks and led their horses to the grass trap. Like the horses, they were tired and hungry and ready for rest. Wilder checked over Rabbit again after setting the heavy panniers on the back porch. The crazy animal led like a lamb now. He didn't have any sap left in him—for Fancy, for humans, for anything.

Red opened the back door and a wave of stale air mixed with mouse smell filled their noses. The old men were tough, but that didn't mean they weren't accustomed to clean homes with feminine touches and large lazy chairs to lean back in at the end of the day. This place promised none of that.

The lights came on, which was a surprise and a big plus. The middle of the trailer was a living room/kitchen, and there was a bedroom on either end. The smaller bedroom had one twin bed and the other had two sets of bunkbeds. There was a couch and a long table with two benches. The couch faced a wood-burning stove in the corner. No TV. Pretty Spartan accommodations.

"Old man Wilhoit didn't spoil his cowboys, did he?" Red commented.

"But the mice seem to have it pretty good," Papa added.

"Can you imagine how many snakes are under this tornado bait?"

Tornado bait, Wilder thought, *that was funny*. He imagined a tornado hunter laying out mobile homes to bring a tornado to his trap, the same way he baited coons back home. Of course, he lived in a trailer back home. It was still funny.

"Just imagine that, Wilber," Red went on. "There's got to be hundreds of the scaly critters under there. Just waiting around for a mouse or your foot to fall through the quarter inch particle board floor we're standing on top of." Red whistled.

"Snakes are just being snakes," Wilder answered and knew it didn't make a lot of sense. It was the best he could come up with. It sounded like something Papa would say. There was no way he was going to let Red get to him.

"You know, if the mice can get in here, which they obviously have, then what would stop a snake from nosing his way in? That'll keep a fella up at night."

Wilder shrugged. But he thought he might get his flashlight out. It wouldn't hurt to check things out under the beds and such, which he did.

Red took kitchen duty, seeing as how this was his trip and he clearly liked to eat. Wilder took his small necessaries bag, along with Papa's and put them in the bunk bed room. Wilder dumped mouse nests that he had found in the dresser off the front porch. One had a collection of pale pink mouse babies squirming. The bathroom was out of commission. The toilet had deep black rings and water stains signifying it had never known a cleaning. The flush handle was unhooked and Wilder was too disgusted to mess with any plumbing fixes. The shower stall was turned off, too.

Great place Red had found them, Wilder thought. Wilder wished they were on the ground somewhere watching a glowing campfire. Sleeping on dirt would have been cleaner than this place.

In the kitchen, Papa was banging on his cell phone. He had retrieved it from the panniers. Wilder had been raised to observe and never ask stupid questions. Or any questions at all, unless it couldn't be helped. Smart people, and good cowboys and carpenters, simply observed closely and figured things out for themselves. But it looked like Papa was having trouble, squinting at the small black device.

"Phone dead, Papa?"

Papa looked up. "I think it's melted."

"Maybe it's just wet."

"It didn't seem to be wet." He handed it to Wilder.

Wilder pried open the plastic flip phone and it was obvious the plastic had sagged on one end. It was melted all right.

"No way," Wilder exclaimed, "this phone got fried by the lightning!"

He showed the melt to Papa. Papa shook his head.

"That's a new one."

Red turned around from the gas stove, which shockingly seemed to be working. He was frying potatoes and summer sausage.

"I thought these potatoes were a little soft when I was cutting them up," Red said.

Wilder picked one up from the grimy counter that Red hadn't bothered to wipe down. It was a little soft.

Papa shook his head.

"Got microwaved a little, I guess." Red laughed and turned back to his hash. He was letting the water run in the sink, the first minute had been solid red rust, and now it was cloudy. Eventually the pressure tank would drain and clean water would return to the old bunkhouse.

"What's the name of this ranch, Mr. Guffey?" Wilder asked as he set the table with paper plates he had found. He placed the bottle of Tabasco sauce he had packed in the middle. Wilder planned to get through whatever kind of cooking might happen on this trip with a little spice.

"It used to be the JA ranch. Goodnight's old place. But it's belonged to the Wilhoit family for as long as I know. They brand with a rafter lazy W. There it is over on that leather piece on the wall.

"I think this place is just used for hunters now. You'd have to be really hard up to live in this place."

When Wilder looked over he saw the framed leatherwork piece that some cowboy must have done years and years before. Next to it was an Ace Reid Cowpoke's cartoon calendar. It was from 1976. The place had clearly been used since then, but the cowboys must have liked seeing the witty cowboy cartoons.

They ate fast, without talking. Wilder had learned to be comfortable in silence from living with Papa. At first, years ago, he had felt it his responsibility, a politeness even, to talk all the time. But he had come to see that was really immaturity, not politeness. Emptyheaded people run their mouths all the time with nothing really to say. Adding Red, a man who liked to talk, to their silence was uncomfortable, but not for long.

The men walked bow-legged and stooped-over after dinner. Their muscles had cooled and tightened up and they looked old and tired. They both popped some aspirin and hobbled off to their bedrooms. Wilder figured they were going down for early bed. He went outside.

The rain was gone now and there was just a glowing sunset to the west over the river. He rubbed down Fancy with handfuls of last year's dead bluestem as she grazed. He saw deer going to the river and listened to three coyote packs howl out their night time plans. A bull-bat roared over his head and spooked him for a second. "Bull-bat tiger shark," Wilder muttered and smiled.

A bull-bat was really a night hawk. The blue jay-sized birds came out at dusk and caught insects by scaring them with the roaring sound their wings made in the wind. Back home, in Colorado, Wilder had told Sunny Parker, his friend who was a girl, about them one time. She said that name didn't make a lick of sense. They weren't bulls or bats. Which was right. So she started calling them bull-bat tiger sharks. Which made even less sense but was funny.

He liked thinking about Sunny.

On the horizon Wilder could see the caprock and on the caprock were dotted red flashing lights from wind turbines. In the few years of Wilder's life he had seen massive new wind farms spring up between his house in Colorado and all across the panhandle. They changed the landscape, which felt wrong to him. The red lights blinked at him now, like a row of lights on a fallen-over Christmas tree.

He pulled the pistol out of his saddle bags and dried it with his dirty but dry shirt. He triple-checked it was unloaded and, alone with the old piece for the first time, couldn't help doing some quick draws with it stuck under his belt.

The knot was out of his stomach. After a day like today, there wasn't any room for knots.

Inside, the old men were barely moving.

Papa wished he had the phone. He was going to call the drive off, have Art come and pick them up. He didn't know if he'd be able to sit in the saddle tomorrow. In 15 minutes of sleep he dreamed that he saw Wilder drown in the river and couldn't save him. He was up all night, mice scurrying around and him going to the porch five times to pee under the stars.

ᴡɢ

CHAPTER NINE

Crow's Feet

Wilder didn't figure the old men would get up early, even they though had a long push to finish the drive today. Still, he arose with the sun like he normally did. Papa and Red were both up drinking coffee in the small kitchen.

Wilder found some toilet paper that had survived the mouse infestation in a steel tin in the bathroom. Previous cowboys and hunters had learned that mice love toilet paper. In the first gray light of dawn Wilder walked to the outhouse in his boots and white underwear with a flashlight. He didn't wear his hat.

The outhouse had a crescent moon carved on the door and a deer antler screwed down for a handle. Inside there was one hole without a white seat and a tin Coors rodeo sign, almost rusted through. Spider webs were everywhere, and Wilder saw black widow eggs hanging in the top right corner with his flashlight beam. He wished he had planned ahead yesterday and cleaned the place out. There was a broom leaning in the corner but it didn't have any bristles left. That must have been for the black widows, Wilder thought.

He shrugged and sat down . . . and heard an immediate rattlesnake buzz beneath him!

He sprang right back up, almost running through the front door and tripping on his underwear. His heart was racing. Seeing a snake in the daylight on the porch was one thing, hearing one close to you in the dark was another. A primal surge of adrenaline and fear coursed through him. He stood there panting in the tall prairie grass next to the outhouse door.

He calmed down and reopened the door. Nothing. Same outhouse. Same old hole with worn places in the wood for two legs. He stepped one foot into the out-house and peered his flashlight over the hole and into the dark depths below.

About five feet down, a big rattler sat in the corner. The snake's tongue flickered in and out, rapidly moni-toring for the smell of a predator or prey. It responded to the light and buzzed its tail, mad at the blinding intrusion above. The outhouse pit was pretty filled up with years of decaying cowboy poop and dirt fall-ing in from the sides. It was a fine home for mice and those that prey on mice. The accumulation of refuse the snake was laying on seemed solid . . . dried hard.

"Holy cow," Wilder whispered out loud, "could that thing have bit my bottom?"

The snake rose its triangle head as if to answer, "You bet."

Wilder had to go to the bathroom. This was a big problem. He had gone outside many times, but felt this problem needed a quick solution. There was no way to whack him with his belt. He went for the pistol.

"There's a big snake in the outhouse," he told the two surprised old men as he burst into the kitchen. "I'm gonna shoot him with the pistol."

"Well . . . hold on," Papa started his response to Wild-er's bold announcement.

Red jumped up. "No, no, I got just the medicine for that," he said quickly, "Come with me, Wilber."

Wilder followed Red to the back porch where he re-trieved his shotgun from his saddle. "Stubby was made for this little job," Red said. He slicked a shell into the chamber with the pump action on the old gun. Wilder begrudgingly left the pistol packed.

The three of them marched out to the outhouse in a line following Wilder's light beam, Papa at the tail, still holding his coffee cup.

Wilder creaked open the door and peered in, followed by Red and his big belly. With the small circle of light Wilder found the big snake, still coiled and now buzzing again. Red squeezed into the outhouse next to Wilder. There wasn't any room for Papa, which was fine with him.

"Oh yeah, he's a big rascal, ain't he?" Red said.

"Yeah, I almost sat on him," Wilder said.

Red broke out laughing. Wilder could hear Papa laughing, too, outside in the dark. "That would have been a bad way to go, son. Here lies Wilber Good, bit on the bum by a buzztail," Red kept laughing as he held the shotgun like a pistol into the hole.

"Well, shoot him," Wilder implored.

"I can't see him good. Hold that flashlight closer to the barrel."

"The hole is too small, I can't see what you're seeing."

"Grab that poop putter and chouse him over to the middle."

Wilder looked at Red, inches away from him in the dark. "Poop putter?"

"The broom," Red replied.

Wilder did as he was told and grabbed the bristleless broom. He stuck it into the hole and the snake buzzed at maximum rpm. Wilder felt him strike the broom bottom with a *thump*. It felt like a pretty good punch and was startling. It was crazy how much power a snake could throw into a bite.

The snake liked the corner and Wilder tried a couple maneuvers while still holding the flashlight, his head and Red's hovering over the hole.

"Why do you call this thing a poop putter?" Wilder asked. He regretted it at once, but he had to know.

"When the stack gets too high, you got to knock it over," Red answered. Wilder had to think about that one for a second, then he got it. *Makes sense*, he thought. His attention returned to the snake.

Wilder and Red adjusted and readjusted the tools they were pointing, trying to get barrel and light on the same place and then on the snake. From outside, Papa asked a thoughtful question, "Is it wet down there?"

"There," Red said, "I got him." They all heard the safety switch off the shotgun with a slight metallic . . . *click*.

"Red, you might not ought to do that," Papa said from the outside as he backed up a step.

BOOM!

The shotgun blast exploded the quiet dark morning in the Red River foothills. It was followed by a wet, gloppy splash.

The snake had been lying on a thin crust of dried rainwater and filth. The shotgun blast hit him square, but also released a violent backsplash up through the outhouse hole and into the peering faces of Wilder and Red. They backed out slowly, hollering like branded calves. From the chest up, they were covered in black sludge.

Papa started crying he laughed so hard. For the second time that week, Wilder and Red started gagging. They quit hollering. Wilder grabbed handfuls of rain and dew-wet grass and wiped his face. Red did the same, trying to keep his lips shut. The sewer smell that had faded with lack of use came roaring back. Putrid aromas filled their nostrils. They couldn't escape from the onslaught.

As Wilder rolled in the grass he had one thought, he was glad he hadn't worn his hat.

After a harsh scrubbing in the fresh water of the stock tank with an old can of Babo laundry soap, Wilder felt a little better. Red had taken a turn, too, baring his hairy, red chest and fat belly to the horses. He had been wearing his only shirt at the time, which was worse for him. It now hung on the back porch to dry.

Red cooked breakfast shirtless, which made it hard to ignore his big belly hanging so far over his belt. He caught Wilder looking.

"Wilber, I'll have you know I wear the same size pants as I did in high school," Red announced.

Papa smirked. Wilder looked at his oatmeal.

"I knew you in high school, remember?" Papa said.

"I do. These Levi's are 34×36s. Same size my mama bought me."

"Yeah, well, that may be true. But what about the inner tube you got hanging down over them?" Papa asked.

"Oh, that," Red smiled big, "that came after. I had a bunch of babies, you know."

Wilder wasn't sure if it was legal to laugh at that, but a big laugh came bubbling up that he couldn't suppress. "Mr. Guffey, you ain't had no babies . . ." Wilder said.

They all started laughing so hard the table shook.

As Wilder wiped some tears from his eyes he noticed the deep creases in the corners of Red's and Papa's eyes. Crow's feet. They weren't ugly and harsh the way most people thought of them but full of laughter and happiness.

Wilder knew you couldn't fake crow's feet. They weren't a tattoo you could buy and wear in false toughness connecting you to something you appreciated. You had to earn them. Wilder had practiced his squinting into the sun and wind and momentary rushing water of West Texas, the same elements that had crafted the canyons and made their mark on Papa's and Red's faces.

Only the deep, rich outdoor life could give you those. It was the patina of time spent in God-breathed beauty. And then, when you got wrinkles that way, they were engraved on your heart, as much as your skin.

He hoped he'd have eyes like theirs when he was 76, sitting around a mouse-infested bunkhouse somewhere on this river.

They laughed and ate and saddled up.

Papa grimaced as he tried to lope out to the south, picking up cows along the way. He hoped his pain tolerance and aspirin supply would hold out. He felt terrible about the lightning storm. In many ways he wanted Wilder to have the same life he had, on the ranch, with all the honor and pride that that life carried. But he also knew how dangerous it could be. There was no risk worth a life, at least not his grandson's life.

But then he argued into the cool morning air that that was exactly why many people raised kids who were sissies and wimps. They didn't want their kids or grandkids to suffer as they had. But all along it was those risks that made people what they were, or weren't.

He and Marian had wrestled back and forth with their Will in this regard. First they had followed ranching tradition and put in a clause that the ranch could only be inherited by Livy or any possible grandkids if they chose to live on the ranch and work it. It could not be sold outright until they had been dead for ten years. They knew inheriting a pile of money, millions of land value dollars, was the death knell to many a good family. Some things weren't for sale at any price.

But then they had changed their minds, softening. Who were they to dictate the lives of their kids—to try to rule past the grave? How selfish was that? He had chosen this life from his dad, as his dad had, too. There had been no son, and Livy was off in Colorado. Why tie her and Hank to a way of life they might not want whole-heartedly?

He couldn't escape the feeling that the land, and perhaps generational land, was valuable, much deeper than money. That working livestock alongside wildlife in open country was vitally important to people, to the world. To him, the struggle and beauty that land ownership represented had always been worth more than the liquidity of cash, and he had been offered an eight-figure payout many times. He couldn't imagine another life. Could it be true that some people really wanted to live in cities, stacked up on top of each other?

He just knew that, for him, staying close to the land, where his food came from and where his body would one day go, was a big piece of his code.

That thought made him feel gratitude more than anything. He didn't know what the right thing was. He spoke out loud to God and said thanks and asked for help to get Wilder home safe. That was enough for today. And then he went back to picking up cows in the foothills.

As Wilder rode, he noticed three or four tarantulas roaming the flat, rocky places. He had seen them before in the hot months, usually July. They were one of God's creatures he couldn't get excited about. His science teacher kept one as a pet at school, and they had a weird smell. Their hairy bodies and the big leather-looking brown spot gave him the creeps. He stepped on them when he could.

But he felt bad about it. He knew he should be better than that. A cowboy shouldn't care about tarantulas. Black widows were everywhere in the panhandle, mainly around houses and barns, and he paid them little mind. They were much more dangerous than a tarantula, he knew. Still, he steered clear when he saw the large, moving black spots horseback.

The herd had stayed together for the most part and were scattered along the river on the south side. Wilder pulled Rabbit along. The burro led smoothly now, if slower. The cowboys had the cows bunched up, rough-counted, and pointed west again in 30 minutes. The horses were in good shape, not having been ridden very hard the day before. Wilder had fed them all handfuls of cow cake he had packed in the panniers. The high protein, molasses-sweetened feed was ·wolfed down quickly.

They pushed along in silence for four hours. They crossed two more pasture gates but still rode on the Rafter Lazy W. Red pulled up when the sun was high and hot, and Wilder figured they would take a lunch on the ground near the river. Red waited for Wilder and Papa at a sandstone outcropping.

Wilder and Papa hobbled their horses, looping the bridles on the saddle horn away from the horses' feet. They grazed.

Wilder noticed that Red still carried an outhouse aroma. He figured he must as well. *Ehhh*, he thought, *I guess you get used to it.*

"Nice bunch of pairs you bought, Red," Papa offered when they came together. "I'm thankful."

"You know the Red Mud doesn't doesn't breed, or keep, any junk," Red replied. "Any wild cattle on that place get sent to the sale barn and Wiley, the manager, has cowboys on those quads every day looking at cattle. He offered to send a few hands on this deal when I mentioned it."

"He would have charged you delivery."

"Yeah, he probably would have."

"That's what makes a good manager."

"That and oil money. And getting rain. Having mailbox money from oil sure makes ranching easy. I think that place is over 50,000 acres."

Wilder leaned back against the sandstone Red and Papa sat on. It was best to keep off the ground at their age. They drank from their canteens, filled at the snake house, and snacked on granola bars and blackened bananas. Rabbit had survived the trip so far but he had been hard on the cargo. Red ate a can of Vienna sausages, tipping the slime off the top for a waiting Coffee. Wilder wasn't picky, but he hated Vienna sausages.

"I asked Wiley when I bought this bunch how many they were running," Red said. Wilder knew this was a major taboo among cowboys and ranch men. A person never asked the acreage or the cow count for a ranch. It was like asking how much money you made or had in the bank. It was deeply rude and showed one to be a greenhorn.

Red paused, sensing the thoughts of Papa and perhaps Wilder.

"Well, I've known Wiley forever and it's not like they're his cows. He's just the manager working for a paycheck." Having explained himself, he continued.

"Still, he kept his cards to his chest. He said, 'Sometimes a few too little, and sometimes a few too many.' Ha—that's about right, isn't it?" Red laughed.

Papa nodded. That was the job of ranching. Conservation. Watching your grass and trying to keep the cow numbers balanced on what the rain delivered. They were just grass salesman, in truth.

"We sure got lucky not having any cows in these pastures, either," Papa said.

"Yeah, I called everybody, but you know how that

goes, I still keep expecting to run into some cows. Which won't be too bad, if we do. We got Wilber and Rabbit with us."

Wilder nodded. He knew he was one of the guys now. Red's ribbing only meant he had risen a notch or two in his eyes.

"My only worry is that these cows are so well-behaved they're walking too slow. We'll be stretching to get home tonight. Course, I'd rather them be slow than chasing them all over tarnation," Red added and popped a couple more pills with a swig of water.

Wilder knew there weren't any other bunkhouses to sleep in between here and there. They were prepared for a night out, having packed the soogans, but Wilder was hoping to make it home. A night on the range sounded fun to him, but his constant worry for the old men had blunted some of his adventurous spirit. He didn't have a good reason to fear for them the way he did. They had done everything perfectly up to this point.

He had no idea their bodies were breaking down.

CHAPTER TEN
Wilder Rides Alone

There was nothing to do but keep pushing, so they packed up their light lunch and remounted. The cows had taken a lunch break, too, and seemed reluctant to stop grazing and nursing calves and continue on.

A half mile later they came to a steep creek drainage that ran into the river from the south. Wilder saw Papa pull up and stop his horse a couple hundred yards ahead, on the flank. Wilder couldn't tell why he had stopped. His instincts told him to stop, too, but the cows were a good ways in front of him, so he kept going.

He crested a small rise and saw it. What Papa had to be looking at. In his mind he could hear Papa saying, "What in the Sam Hill is that?"

On the other side of the creek drainage stood a bull buffalo.

Wilder shook his head a bit. *Can't be a buffalo*, he thought. He looked back at Papa who had turned his horse toward Wilder at a walk but was still looking at the buffalo.

"That is a buffalo," he murmured to himself. The bull was broadside to the herd that was about to walk up the rise in the land. He was massive, with a head that must have weighed 500 pounds. The thick chocolate fur curled and boiled off his head and down his back. A large piece of blond winter wool flapped in the breeze on his rear haunch. Shiny black horns poked out of his head.

Wilder's mind went to Indian buffalo hunts. When the Comanches had run these animals down with lances and speared them from horseback. He didn't think he would try it, but he considered how difficult it must have been. If only he had an obsidian spear point . . .

The bull turned and curled his lip up, smelling the cows and calves. He grunted, and it sounded like a bear. It was a low rumble that echoed out from deep in his chest. In the silence of the river bottom, Wilder heard it clearly from a hundred yards away.

The cows heard it, too. They all stopped in unison and raised their heads. Fancy's ears pointed up and Rabbit set back on the lead rope. The herd went from lazy and slow to electric.

The bull stepped down hill toward the cows. He had something in his ears. It looked orange. He bellowed again and curled his lip up. When he shook his head rapidly back and forth, the lead cow turned tail.

"Oh boy," Wilder said nervously to Fancy. The bull's advance and the lead cow's turn spread panic in the herd like a grassfire. The cows shot directly toward Wilder in a rush like water.

Wilder dropped Rabbit's lead and threw his hands up, hollering "Whooo . . . cows, Whooo . . . cows!" He reined Fancy to the right to cut off the first cows attempting to break out from the gather. When he went right another bunch cut left, and in three seconds the peaceful cows were spilled. Wilder reined over to them, loping back in the direction they had started the trip from for the first time. Papa and Red came up and tried equally useless movements to keep the cattle bunched.

The bull came trotting right through them, bellowing. Wilder turned to face the bull, thinking maybe that should be his concern now that the cows were raising dust in ten different directions. If he could get this bull out of here, maybe they could get the cows bunched up again.

Fancy pranced under Wilder, which she seldom did. Wilder could tell she was tight, nervous about this new animal with the strange sounds and smell. She humped up, ready for action. Wilder grabbed the horn with his off hand.

The bull lumbered toward him and Wilder hollered, "Hey bully . . . hey! Get out of here!" as he popped his reins on his chaps. The bull kept coming. Wilder touched his spurs to Fancy to try a false charge that sometimes worked on cattle. Fancy made a little crow hop forward and covered ten yards before Wilder put on the brakes again.

The bull was 20 yards out and Wilder could see the tags he wore in each ear clearly. The bull stuck out his big black tongue and licked the snot off his nostrils. *Gosh, he's huge*, Wilder thought. He knew from books that they were famous for being able to turn on a dime.

He had also been taught the old farm wisdom of "Never trust anything with testicles." The only rule with bulls had always been that they were unpredictable.

Wilder's courage melted. Or perhaps wisdom won out. He touched the reins to Fancy's neck to peel out of the way as the buffalo loped past. Fancy took the cue. The buffalo lifted his huge head and threw a hooking black-polished horn their direction even though they were yards away. Fancy kicked back with both hooves like she had at Rabbit yesterday. Wilder held on for the buck. She nicked the bull on the side as he rumbled past, completely unimpressed with cowboys. The bull's flank jumped sideways a foot as a patch of winter hide flew off, but he kept on his path toward the fleeing cows.

Wilder sat and looked around at the blown-up herd, breathing hard all of a sudden. Half of them were out of sight, as were Papa and Red. That wasn't a big surprise in canyon country, which offered ever-present gullies and ridges to hide in. Still, Wilder wondered what to do.

He got off his horse and took his hat off. Sweat had soaked his hair and made another line on the outside of his felt hat. He knew the first thing to do was not panic. Like Papa said, the whole place was fenced. Where could the cattle go?

Except, of course, the buffalo had clearly wrecked some fences getting in here. Wilder picked a strand of windmill grass and stuck the sweet end in his mouth. Fancy was too keyed up to graze. "Easy girl, easy mama," he told her and stroked her neck. Rabbit stood about 20 yards behind them. He wasn't spooked in the slightest. A bull buffalo doesn't really compare to a lightning bolt.

That buffalo must be escaped from the park, he thought. He had never been to Caprock Canyons but knew what it was. They had seen it on the drive in. It was a huge state park that held Colonel Goodnight's old buffalo herd. Hundreds of them. They must be due north of the place right now. Wilder had read a pamphlet on the buffalo at the Turkey motel yesterday and seen a map of the park. He didn't know anything about handling buffalo, except what he had learned in the last three minutes. It was startling.

He looked down and saw the tuft of buffalo wool Fancy had loosened from the bull. He walked over and picked it up. It smelled like cows and dust but had another aroma. It reminded him of Yellowstone and picking up buffalo wool there. He used that wool as a string silencer on the bow he had bought last year. He had hunted mule deer with it at Thanksgiving.

Wilder stuffed the wool in his pants pocket, happy

to have found it. He still didn't know what to do, but he needed to be doing something. He looked around for Coffee, but she had apparently stayed with Papa. Surely she couldn't keep up for long with the kind of riding they were doing now.

He decided to tie Rabbit up on the river, and then work downstream and try and pick up some cows. Red had said this was a huge pasture and Wilder didn't want to get lost or hurt away from the water. The foothills and canyons were a maze that could hide a downed man for weeks.

But then he thought that getting as high as possible might be the first move. He could spot cows and not be wandering blind. The gentle cows they had been pushing would probably be eager to be herded back up and talked to by the cowboys that had been directing them. The grass was good everywhere this year, and the cows would eat as soon as they stopped feeling pressure.

Wow, a real buffalo out here . . . Wilder couldn't get the image out of his mind. After tying Rabbit to a large mesquite near the flood plain, he trotted Fancy south to the largest foothill before the canyons started getting deep and dark coming off the flat Llano caprock. Fancy climbed, and he soon saw 20 of the cows a mile downriver, stopped and staring at a cow in the river. Her legs had disappeared in the mud.

"Great, now we have a cow in the quicksand," Wilder muttered to Fancy. A cow in danger became job number one. He decided to keep Fancy to a walk for the mile to the cattle so he wouldn't spook them any further.

The 20-odd cows and calves were spread out. Two cows stood on the bank grass looking at the stuck cow. She was in a big sandy wash without any tracks. The buffalo drama must have pushed her into the sand. She called to the cows on the bank and occasionally tried to lift a hind foot out but soon gave up.

Wilder walked Fancy in, quietly calling the cows and assuring them of his good intentions. They spread out for him but didn't leave. The cow in the mud panicked and started bucking up and down to get out. Wilder swung down and stared at her.

He hobbled Fancy, and she grazed while Wilder stared at the cow. This was a bigger problem than he had first thought. A mature cow weighed well over a thousand pounds and was unbelievably strong, but that weight and muscle worked against them when they were high-centered in quicksand. He thought to rope her around the neck and pull with Fancy, but that would immediately choke her air and blood flow.

Some horns would be helpful, but Angus hadn't had horns for a hundred years.

He wished Papa was there. Surely he had been through this a dozen times. Wilder didn't recall ever hearing about it, though. He stepped out onto the sand with one foot. The ground jiggled. Water rose up around his boot. He put some weight on it and it held him. He had been on the river before and knew it would be very unusual for quicksand to swallow his foot, as he only weighed a little more than a hundred pounds. Still he didn't need to die next to a cow.

He put eight steps together toward the cow and spoke to her. She bucked and panicked in short bursts and then resigned herself to cruel death when she tired. But Wilder wasn't a predator and only petted her and spoke softly to her, saying, "Good mama, good mama." He dug in the soupy sand around under her front legs, thinking maybe he could pass his rope and pull around her middle, but it was impossible. Her legs and belly were too swamped.

He decided to whack her a bit to spook her out of the mud on her own power. He tried to explain this to her, feeling bad for making friends only to have to immediately reverse course. Maybe real friendship was always that way, equal parts encouraging and prodding. He ripped down a green mesquite branch, broke off the thorns, and tip-toed back to the cow. He whipped her side over and over again. She bellowed and bucked. On the first jumps it seemed like she made some clearance, but the mud quickly sucked her back down. She didn't sink any lower. Wilder soon quit, the effort pointless. The cow panted with her mouth open. She was close to spent.

Wilder went back to the shore and fretted about roping her. It was going to be ugly . . . pulling on the head of a stuck and helpless cow. Ranchers spent their lives raising cows for food. Every cow here would at some point be sent to the packing house and be processed for a hundred products from leather boots to hamburger patties, and yet their care when on the ranch was almost like a family. They must not suffer or be treated poorly. It was a paradox. It was love.

Wilder felt that love, and it produced worry and grief. Which produced action. He steeled his feelings and shook out a loop. He used his poly calf rope, not the reata, since he was afraid it might break with the dead pull. A reata was a piece of art, not a winch.

She was an easy catch, and Wilder said out loud to her, "Mama, I apologize," before turning Fancy and dallying his rope around the saddle horn. Fancy felt the end pull tight and waited for the spurs.

Wilder spurred and heard the cow gargle as she tried to bellow before the rope cut off her wind. He grimaced at the sound and spurred Fancy harder. The cow made a jump forward into the taut rope and surprisingly her two front feet crested the mud. Wilder reined Fancy back to give slack.

The cow's neck shrunk back to normal size and she laid her head on the sand. She looked about dead. Wilder knew a human would never survive a pull like that. But her front feet were out. Wilder gave her a minute to pant and remember that she was alive. He thought maybe he could whack her again now and save her another neck pull.

But then he realized that was silly. The rope had worked, and her head hadn't popped off, so he stayed with it. One more big pull. He pulled his dally and gathered rope to get closer to the cow. He saw all the other cows and calves staring at him with rapt attention.

He pulled the rope tight again, looked back, and spurred forward, determined not to quit until he felt her release. Fancy buried her four hooves in the rain wet ground and pulled as her partner directed. Her massive chest and hindquarter muscles rippled and the old horse strained against the upward pull of the saddle horn. The cow's neck and head looked grotesque. He thought surely he had killed her.

But Wilder was committed and tickled Fancy with his spurs back and forth and, surprisingly, the cow slipped from the earth with loud sucking sound.

Wilder pulled his dallies quickly and slipped off and ran to the cow. She was out and laying on her side. He pulled the rope from her head and massaged her neck. He told her he was sorry again.

He rubbed her, and Fancy watched, and slowly the cow's eyes blinked and she closed her mouth and blew a burst of air in and then out of her huge boogery nose. Wilder sat with her for a full minute. Then the cow rolled up and got her hind legs under her. Wilder backed up. Her front legs came up and she wobbled forward, and Wilder said, "Good girl," so pleased with himself.

And then the cow charged him.

Wilder saw it coming and dove to the side. The cow put her head down and bucked toward him with a head swipe that held memories of when all cows had horns. Maybe when they were buffalo. Wilder felt his hand pop as he fended off her charge and rolled in the grass. The cow didn't return to fight, lumbering off in a trot to the awaiting, reduced herd.

Wilder jumped back up and hollered, "You're welcome!" when he saw that the cow only had a little fight in her. He was angry for a second, then laughed. He understood the score. She was just doing what good cows do—fight off predators. He was mature enough not to expect the animal to reason. She was still a cow, despite all those mushy feelings he had had earlier. Anger was for small minds, a weakness that seldom produced anything valuable. Wilder had observed that cowboys who got angry with livestock were always the worst cowboys.

When he grabbed the saddle horn with his left hand to get back on Fancy he felt a stabbing pain. He looked at his hand and his left pinky was poked out in a funny direction. He tried to make a fist. Pain coursed through him and he shouted, "Owww!"

The pinky was dislocated. The cow's head must have caught him as he leaped out the way and fended her off. The same thing had happened in a basketball game once in seventh grade. The doctor had popped it back in three days later without any medication. It had been the worst pain of his life. The thought of it now made him queasy.

The muddy cow was now being licked by two other cows, and her calf had found her after several calls back and forth. He slurped the large teats covered in red mud and sand. Milk frothed at the side of his mouth. Milk sounded good to Wilder. *Cold milk*, he thought, standing there holding his hand.

He walked Fancy over to where Rabbit was tied. *What to do?* he thought.

He hadn't been scared until now, but he felt it percolating in his gut. It had been over an hour since the buffalo fiasco. Should he ditch the cows and ride, looking for Papa and Red? They might be hurt and down somewhere. He might be their only chance.

Should he just stay put? He could probably keep the cows in the general vicinity by himself. What good was that, when he didn't have half the herd?

What if it got dark and he was alone? Should he just ride to a road and take the road to a house for help? That seemed childish. He was a cowboy. He could handle himself out here. He had food and water as much as the cows and horses did.

But what about his hand? That was worse. The throbbing and swelling had started. His other fingers and thumb were still usable, but he knew from prior experience that the dislocated pinky was hanging out there like an exposed nerve. It could catch on anything, and when it did the white lights would flash in his eyes.

He couldn't cowboy in the wilderness with a pinky like that. He was going to have to set it. He shuddered.

That was when Wilder remembered something Sunny had said.

CHAPTER ELEVEN

Tough It Out

Wilder couldn't help but think of Sunny as his girlfriend, although both their families made it clear that middle school was still too young for relationship nonsense.

Still, Wilder loved her. He told her that once, on the trip he was now thinking of. They had gone fishing with Gale on the Rio Grande south of town and had to spend the night in the woods when Gale broke his leg. Sunny had helped slow Wilder down and forced him to make good decisions. She had said, "Make good *little* decisions." She explained that all those good little decisions would eventually amount to good big decisions. It was something her dad had taught her.

Sunny couldn't help him now, but her words and strong, dirty face still spoke to him. A terrifying short story by Jack London, *To Build a Fire*, flashed into his mind. In that story a man froze to death by making a long string of terrible little decisions. There was no happy ending to save him.

OK. Sunny, what's the next good little decision? Wilder asked himself.

He was cowboying and so he needed to see to the cows. Papa and Red might be back any second, and he wanted to be ready for them. He was sure they could handle themselves, or just die happy in the pasture, like Papa had mentioned before they left. He decided it would be cowardly to assume weakness on their behalf and seek to help them when he had no reason to believe they were hurt. Those two were rough as cobs.

So he turned and faced his own problems.

He dug in his saddle bags and found his first aid kit. It had been used repeatedly on his recent backpacking trip, so it was well stocked now. There simply wasn't a good way to wrap his pinky, since it stuck out so far from his hand and couldn't be used, but he did the best he could by stuffing a large ball of gauze between the pinky and his index finger and wrapping them together. The bandage made the finger ache, but at least he wouldn't catch it on anything. Any heroic thoughts he had about popping it back into place faded as he touched it.

Then he wrote a note and decided to leave it with Rabbit tied on the river. If he had to follow the cows a ways, the burro would be a sign post for Papa and Red or anyone else looking for him. He didn't need all the food anyway, and maybe Papa and Red would need some. He ripped a blank back page out of his poetry book in his saddle bags. He wrote,

Papa or Red,

I am staying with the cows. My count is 21 cows and 18 calves. The buffalo went east with you guys. I have food and am leaving Rabbit for you guys to eat. Not the burro, the packed food. You know what I mean. I am going to keep my herd together and if they move west I will stay with them. I won't leave this pasture. I'll see ya when I see ya.

Don't shoot into any outhouses if you come across them.

wg

Wilder giggled. That was funny. It was sickening but funny, and it seemed like a long time ago even though it was only that morning. It occurred to Wilder that that was code talk, like Papa had told him about. The ability to laugh in the face of hardship and trials was an essential cowboy skill. Maybe the first skill needed. Maybe the only really necessary skill in the end.

It was code.

He stowed the note in an empty water bottle and tied it to the top of the packsaddle.

Wilder threw a few cans of chili in his saddle bags. After letting Rabbit drink from the river, Wilder tied him hard and fast to a large cedar tree on the riverbank. No one would miss the strange looking animal if they cast a glance down the valley. Satisfied that he was doing the right thing, he swung up on Fancy one-handed and starting walking south to make a big loop around the cows.

An hour of hard riding—it felt good not having to yank Rabbit along anymore—and the cows were back together. They had moved west at least half a mile and Rabbit could no longer be seen, hidden behind bluffs along the winding river. Wilder knew he couldn't keep the cows still, so he got behind them and eased them along making big sweeps along the drag and hoping the lead cow stayed straight down the valley.

The land started to change from the big foothills they had been in for the last ten miles to deeper canyons closer to the river. Wilder expected this, knowing Palo Duro canyon was about 20 miles ahead of them. It was the second biggest canyon in the U.S., after the Grand Canyon. There were more cedars along the banks now. The brushy, green trees made the country feel closer and reduced how far you could see.

Red had said this was the biggest pasture they would pass through, but he hadn't said how big it might be. Papa's pastures were anywhere from two to three sections, a section being 640 acres. In canyon country, that was enough land to get an army lost in. The Comanches had been good at that maneuver. Wilder hoped he would find the fence soon and be able to keep the cattle bunched near it. He could also quit moving further from Papa and Red.

It was still and humid from yesterday's rain and he and Fancy both had a sweat soaking their bodies. Fancy's sweat had foamed up on her chest where the breast collar hung. She hadn't quit, however. She still stepped out with a gait that told the rider she was always ready. Wilder patted her on the shoulder and his hand stuck as their sweat mixed.

The cows were walking in the right direction, but it was now impossible to keep them off the river. Without Red to hold them in check, the cows naturally wandered to the flattest land where walking was easiest. Wilder didn't want to tackle the sandy bottom routinely, so he was forced to let them go. As long as they were slowly moving west he was content.

Wilder watched the cows test the river bottom and then nose their way across the water. He was nervous when Fancy took her first step in cow tracks. He knew if she sunk there would be no way to save her. A bridge would have been nice.

He thought about Papa's advice—*observe the land*. He looked at the banks on either side. There were deer trails and old cows trails that wore down the bank to bare dirt. He studied these and when all the cows had passed and he was sure of his path, he let Fancy choose her own steps. Her big hooves splashed in the deep parts and she lowered her head and drank.

Soon he had crossed and was on solid ground again. He followed the cows up the wide creek bed.

Hours later the fence hadn't appeared and his two Nalgene bottles were about dry. He figured this pasture might be over 10,000 acres. He had heard of pastures on the big ranches being that size. The cows were on the north side of the river now, which wasn't a big deal. He hoped for a windmill which would give him clean water and a place to stop. Drinking from the river, while it appeared clean and cool, seemed like an instant stomach problem. He didn't need to compound his problems. Good little decisions . . .

Of course, heat stroke and dehydration would be a big problem, too. He might have to boil water.

Except now that he thought of it, he hadn't brought the coffee pot.

The sun had begun its descent, and Wilder figured it was past five, maybe six. It was still hot, and the only wildlife he saw were a flock of five or six tom turkeys in a soapberry motte. They watched him as he passed, too hot to even eat the plentiful grasshoppers. One bird was dusting itself in the shaded sand.

His pinky ached. It was like a thorn that had swelled the skin around it and was ready to be expelled. Wilder knew how to fix the problem, too, but didn't think he had the courage to do so. *Tough it out*, he thought.

But it's time to stop, Wilder reflected. Papa and Red hadn't found him quickly, and he was only getting further and further from them with each minute that passed. The cows had taken a meandering right turn off the river at a dry creek junction. Following the creek bed wasn't a bad idea. Most of these creeks came out of box canyons that usually had a spring. If not a spring, at least a dirt tank. Tank water would probably be as good as any to boil, which Wilder decided he could do, if slowly, when he emptied a chili can of its contents.

The fresh rain might have left puddles, too. He had always kind of wanted to sip water from one, like a Texas Ranger. It didn't kill Goodnight, he figured.

The cows moved up the drainage and the steep banks of canyon bluffs rose quickly on each side. Papa's ranch was put together about the same way, and Wilder felt as comfortable in this drainage, as any. He saw lots of sandhill plum thickets, and many still had their bright red plums waiting for the picking. That was good. Wilder could come back for them or wait for more further up.

The creek canyon hollowed out a couple hundred yards in, and Wilder saw a dam that would certainly have water behind it. The cows went around the dam and he saw five ducks fly up. *Good sign*, he thought.

When he crested the dam, Wilder looked for baby ducks but didn't see any.

The dirt tank was at least an acre. He stayed back to let the cows drink. Half the mama cows waded into the water belly deep and drank and stood around like fat hippos. He saw one empty its intestines into the water, the green slime making a loud splashing sound as it dropped a foot from her backside into the pond. Another one let loose a hot stream of yellow pee from under her raised black tail.

"So that's what I have to drink tonight?" he wondered out loud. A mockingbird answered him from the top of a big native elm that grew on the tank's bank. A small scattering of cottonwoods rustled slightly in the breeze. He noted coyote and coon tracks along the bank, along with numerous deer hooves.

Wilder took off his hat and pulled a crispy old leaf from the front of the sweat band. He plucked a fresh green heart-shaped cottonwood leaf and put it where the old one had stained his liner brown. The hat felt cool now. It was a little native air-conditioning Papa had showed him when he was young. He was old enough to know that most of the effect was mental—but then, he was old to enough to know that most things were mental anyway.

Like sleeping out by yourself all night.

The cows drank for 30 minutes and milled around the canyon. Its far end kept going and, twisting, got lost in tall cedar trees and a few big cottonwood tops. Wilder pushed the cows up and walked Fancy belly deep in the cool water. She splashed and sucked water in and out of her nose like a two-year-old at bath time. Then Wilder both felt and heard her add her contribution of urine to the still pond.

Wilder needed a drink. He needed some food, too. His belly felt hollowed out and, like the metaphor he had read in several books, was gnawing on his backbone. He steered clear of the antelope jerky. It was good, but he knew the hot, salty meat would wreck him right then. He pushed the cows a hundred yards past the pond and went back for the plums.

The plum thicket was about five feet high. He hobbled Fancy and took his two water bottles to fill with fruit. He picked the unusually large, red plums, about half the size of an apricot, and ate the first 20. He sucked each plum down to the sour pit and kept a few of those in his cheek as he went. The hit of sugar and water instantly soothed his thirst and hunger.

It was easy to fill both bottles, and he returned to the tank better off. Many calves had bedded down in the tall ungrazed grass. He felt like a good cowboy. The herd was content and stood a good chance of staying in the general vicinity for the night that he seemed destined to spend with them.

As long as no buffalo showed up.

For a second, Wilder became scared thinking of the buffalo and spending a night out here alone. He had never soloed before. He had spent plenty of nights in the backyard by himself, but that hardly counted, not for a 13-year-old. A part of him was excited for the challenge; another part of him wished this hadn't happened.

He felt like a calf needing to bed down and be close to a mother. That was his next job: find a campsite.

Finding campsites was Wilder's specialty, as he considered it. That thought brought him out of the fear and doubt and set him to work; shelter, chop wood, make food.

The very worst thing that could happen to him would be to lose Fancy and be afoot. She probably wouldn't run off, especially in new country like this, although he had heard that stock always knew where their home range was. Still, he would let the horse graze hobbled until nightfall and then would tie her up the canyon but still close to him. He figured he could rig a "highline" that would be more comfortable for her. Gale had showed him how in the mountains.

He figured the big elm by the cottonwood grove would be his best bet for a campsite. The cows would have to come through him to leave, and the tree would shelter him from light rain or wind. Wildlife would undoubtedly come to the water in the night and crunch around and wake him, but at least the water gave him one side that would be protected. After hobbling Fancy and unsaddling her, he cleared a spot under the elm.

He gathered a large pile of wood, an all night pile, from dead mesquite and a hackberry grove nearby. Cracking the limbs and dragging them proved to be very difficult with the wounded hand. Sometimes Wilder had to use his whole body to push against the heavy limbs. But the brittle, dry wood broke eventually and Wilder started a fire, even though it was still hot.

He had packed three different sources of fire. With Big and Corndog he had considered himself the Fire King.

He needed water most, but had to empty a chili can before he could boil any. He grabbed a can from his saddlebags draped across a low branch on the elm.

"Vienna sausages . . ." he muttered out loud with disgust. He grabbed the other two cans. Both were Vienna sausages. Wilder hated Vienna sausages. These were large cans that Red must have packed. Wilder must have grabbed them by mistake in his haste at the river.

They were standard wilderness food, but Wilder detested the slimy pink tubes. He rolled a can in his good hand and read the ingredients out of spite. He knew what they were made of; mechanically separated chicken, beef, pork . . . garlic powder . . . and a bunch of chemicals. The worst part was the clear gelatinous gravy that rested on the top of the sausages inside the can. He knew he should be thankful for the protein, but he couldn't help being disgusted with Red for packing them and with himself for not paying attention.

Wilder had cut up lots of animals to eat. He knew the chicken, beef, and pork parts that were fine ground to make these sausages were all the things he generally threw to the buzzards . . . like organs, guts, lips, and butts. It was kind of a funny joke until you were stuck with them.

He emptied a water bottle of the precious plums and laid them on a saddle blanket. Then he used the small P-38 can opener that Papa had given him. He had said it was from his service in WWII. The garlic aroma hit him in the hot afternoon air and his hunger evaporated.

He plucked the short meat sticks out of the can one by one and dropped them into the water bottle for later. He rinsed the can numerous times and scrubbed it with sand to get as much flavor out as possible. Of course, there were other flavors he had to worry about.

He searched the pond edge for the clearest water he could find. He imagined he found some with green algae growing under it, without any floating cow manure. He tried not to think of all the dead fish and birds and turtle poop that would be on the bottom of the pond. He filled the can and sat it on a coal bed near the fire.

Over the next two hours he walked up the bluff and checked the river for cattle or cowboys three times, built a lean-to under the elm, boiled water to fill one water bottle, started a poem in his head about horses drinking windmill water that he would write later, and wondered constantly whether he had the guts to pop his finger back into place.

The tepid boiled water tasted awful and he understood why old-time cowboys drank mostly coffee. Coffee could cover up the brackish taste of old water with years of rotting organic matter in it. He got the good idea to crush plums into the water, and that was a big improvement. A huge improvement. Prune juice.

The canyon had covered the pond and his little fire with shadow now. Wilder couldn't see the sunset, the canyon was too deep, but he watched the sky turn orange and then purple over him.

As he sat stone still at the pond a roadrunner appeared and started chasing grasshoppers. The arrow-like bird darted back and forth in humorous fashion after the bugs. Wilder had seen videos of them killing rattlesnakes, which was an unbelievable feat for a small bird. After more than ten kills, including one lizard, the bird ran off again, its head down and head crest up. A near flightless bird. A survivor. A warrior.

Maybe he could eat grasshoppers too? Observe the land, Papa had said.

He still hadn't eaten the Viennies. *What did Vienna, Austria, have to do with these cheap little sausages, anyway?* he thought. *Wasn't that a place for operas? Did Europeans go to operas and eat slimy, cheap sausage?* He had two reasons not to eat them. The first was that they were gross, staring at him from across the fire in a piled up sludge at the bottom of his Nalgene. The second reason was that he didn't want to throw them up when he clamped down on his pinky and squeezed.

His first pinky dislocation had happened last year. As his mom, Livy, watched, the doctor had calmly pulled a pen out of his shirt pocket while he talked to Wilder about his basketball season. Wilder was looking the man in his bearded face while he softly probed Wilder's busted hand with his own soft, small hands. He interviewed Wilder casually, like he was just checking things out and getting details about the injury. The doctor put him at ease and Wilder figured a nice nurse would show up with pain meds or a shot to deaden his hand.

But the doctor had slid his pen between Wilder's pinky and index finger and, before Wilder knew what was happening, the man squeezed the two fingers violently, leveraging the pinky over the pen body.

The result was electric pain. Wilder had instinctively tried to pull back, but the doctor held the fingers together like some kind of mad man in a torture chamber. Wilder had been taught not to cry or howl, but he groaned as the current shot through him. He felt the blackness coming . . . and the joint slipped back into place.

The doctor released the hand and Wilder's knees felt squishy. The memory faded after that but he remembered thinking he wanted to take a swing at the man. The doctor had just smiled and left the room.

Wilder still wished he had punched him. But the terrible experience with the smiling assassin doctor gave him a road map to fix his hand now. He felt he had to. He had to get it done—before the swelling got worse, before he could finish the drive, before he could eat. He felt shaky, committing to the decision he had been playing with all day.

He sat down beside the pond and removed his bandage brace and soaked the hand. The hot, angry swelling disappeared in the dark water. It felt good and eased some of the pain. He played in the sandy mud and the pressure and coolness took away some of the throbbing and fear inside of him.

He took a pen-sized three-inch cottonwood stick that he had carved earlier with his Mooremaker knife from behind his ear. He stuck both hands down in the mud and water. He put the stick between the two fingers.

It had to be like branding cattle, he thought. You had to go all the way. Commit to it. Pulling teeth. Punching Boone in seventh grade. If you were going to do it, you had to jump in. Head first. Do or die. Eye of the tiger.

He gritted his teeth and prepared for the pain.

He squeezed the fingers around the stick . . . and then fell over.

Later, he realized he was alive when he felt an animal licking his face.

ᗯᘓ

CHAPTER TWELVE

Fix His Wagon

When the herd spooked, Papa and Red hadn't. They had never herded buffalo, but a deeply boyish sense of adventure was awakened in the men at the sight of the old bull. This would be another story to tell, another page in their long cowboy histories of wild times. It was going to mess up the drive, but it was thrilling.

They both kicked their horses into a lope, curled back wide, and took positions on high bluffs where they could watch the action and stay in sight of each other. Posting up on bluffs and making yourself visible to the next man on the drive was old cowboy practice and they both followed it instinctually.

The action didn't gather cattle, however, and from what they saw it was going to be a long day. Half of the cows were heading back to the east in front of the buffalo, running for their home pasture. Papa was surprised they didn't stop—at least from what he could see in the rugged country.

Papa saw that Wilder was fine and had half the herd. He figured the boy could hold them while he and Red regathered the other bunch. He didn't look forward to it, but he knew that was all there was to be done. He started making tracks east.

After a couple miles he saw the buffalo on the river bottom. He was standing in the mud and flinging wet sand up over his back. Papa admitted the big bull was a beautiful sight. It was like being in a time machine. If Quanah Parker and a band of Comanches appeared over the next hill, he wouldn't have been surprised.

Another couple miles and he saw a bunch of calves

and then three cows. He gathered them from the foot-hills and took them to the river. Red showed up with another cow.

It was hot and both men were about out of water. Papa's seat was hurting and a headache had started from the dehydration. They both swung down off their saddles and let the horses drink. Coffee trotted up beside Papa and stood in the water, chest deep. She drank and looked at the men with her ears up and her big red tongue panting.

"I didn't know I was getting a herd of beefaloes," Red said, disgusted. He was too tired and sore to have much humor at the moment. "But that was a quite a sight."

"Yes, it was," Papa agreed. "But, this little rodeo just got a lot harder," he added, stating the obvious, which was something he never did.

"You OK, old buddy?" Red looked at him with concern.

Papa sat on the bank and looked at the trickle of the Red River at his feet.

"When's the last time you drank outta here?"

"Long time, I guess. We used to all the time. I guess we got smart at some point." Red knew they were both out of water with a hot sweaty task looming in front of them.

"You got any aspirin?" Papa asked.

"No, my meds are with the burro."

"Mine, too. You need your meds?" Papa asked, unaware of any specific needs Red might have.

"Not really, but I have some blood pressure pills I'm supposed to take. They're no big deal, it's just that if I don't have them," Red laughed, "I'll die."

Papa's eyes opened wide in concern.

"And then you'll have to pack my heavy carcass out

like a mule deer." Red laughed again. "What meds you take?" he asked Papa.

"Oh, nothing. But I have to drink and I didn't see any windmills or solar wells in this pasture."

Papa washed his hands in the gentle flow and let the dirty water from the hand-washing drift down, then he lifted a splash of water to his face and rubbed it back and forth across his short gray hair. He tested the water on his lips. It was "gyppy" like he remembered, from the heavy salt and gypsum deposits in the caprock. He took a big drink on the second scoop. *Not bad*, he thought. The water was cool, and it replenished him. He thought about being home in his lazy chair for an afternoon nap.

Red filled his canteen by submerging it and took long drinks that ran down his shirt front. His red chest hair was visible through his soaked white shirt.

"Well, we got ourselves in a hell of a mess, Wendell," Red said after drinking a full canteen and refilling it.

"Yeah," Papa acknowledged. "Best case, we'll catch the rest in the next couple miles and catch up with Wilder this evening."

"The boy will be all right?"

"He's pretty savvy. He may get lonesome, but he isn't dumb. He won't do anything risky. Livy said he just spent ten days on a campout with two buddies."

Red was surprised. "Why did he want to do that?"

Papa chuckled, "I don't know. Kind of like moving this stupid herd of cows."

"Just to see if he could do it?" Red recognized the irony.

"Something like that," Papa said as he swung up and Red followed. "We're about to find out aren't we?"

Papa noticed that Coffee had disappeared sometime after they left their watering stop. He figured she would show back up; she always did. The ground was soft from the rain, making the cows easy to track. Whenever a set of hoofprints wandered off the bottom Red or Papa would follow it and return the cow or calf to the river.

They worked in the foothills, riding over the same tracks they had made earlier in the day. It wasn't long before they saw the bunkhouse trailer and the outhouse and cows lined up on the fence. A few wires were down, and it looked like several cows had jumped the fence and were heading home. They counted 15 cows and 22 calves. They had no idea how many were with Wilder and how many had jumped the fence.

The sun was falling already by about six o'clock, but there was nothing to do but push the cows back west. If they'd had their cell-phones they might have called Art to pick them up and bring trailers. But even then, Wilder would still be out there holding the herd, and there was no way they were going to abandon him.

Papa had pushed himself just about as far as he could go. He had never hit a wall like this before. It wasn't that he thought he was still the man he was at 40, it was that usually he was wise enough to stay out of situations that demanded so much of his body. His seat was on fire, and now that the cows were caught he dismounted to walk a bit.

He chewed some granola bars and led Bud behind him. Red rode over when the cows were basically pointed west and moving. Their spook and fight were gone, too.

"Wendell, why don't you go back to the bunkhouse and sleep. We can call this stupid deal off. I'll go find Wilber and bring him home, and we'll eat and sleep and shoot rattlesnakes till midnight."

"No, you know I can't leave my grandson out there. I'll be all right. I just have to walk a ways. Bud's tired."

Red got down and led his horse next to Papa. The two old mens' spurs clinked and sang as they waded across the native pasture.

They walked and snacked on food from their saddlebags and were silent. The cows stayed in the river bottom and herded quietly like sheep.

They rested often, more often than they would have figured they needed to, sitting on rocks and high banks in the floodplain. Dusk set in, and they knew they would have stopped hours ago if Wilder hadn't been up ahead somewhere. They needed to stop and they both knew it, but neither wanted to be the first to bring it up.

Then they saw the buffalo again.

He was off to the right, on the north side of the river. The cows were just black blobs in the dusk now. The buffalo grunted and growled his deep call and the cows froze.

Red jumped in the saddle immediately.

"I'll fix his wagon," he said out loud as he evened up his reins. Papa was tightening his cinch. Red pulled out Stubby.

"What are you gonna do, Red?"

Red spurred his horse off but hollered over his shoulder, "Fix his wagon, like I said."

Papa snorted and swung up. His joints and muscles had tightened and the saddle seat felt like a 55-gallon drum with a fire burning on the inside. Red was loping across the river straight toward the buffalo. Papa stayed back to hold the cows in case they broke east again.

Red was riding like a jockey in a horse race into the gray dusk, whipping and spurring. Mud flew from Burrito's hooves as he drove the gelding across the river and into the foothills. He had the shotgun in his right hand, reins in the left.

BOOM! A hundred yards from the buffalo, he fired.

The short black shotgun barrel blew flame out two feet into the evening. Burrito hopped left at the huge noise close to his head, but kept his line. Red jacked another shell in with his rein hand.

The buffalo spun around and perked his ears up from his insolent staring at the cows. His eyes focused on the wild fat man riding a horse toward him, but he wasn't ready to run.

Red closed the distance and fired again.

BOOM! The shotgun threw its fire and smoke and cloud of lead toward the 15-hundred-pound animal.

"Get out of here!" Red hollered, spurring Burrito in a mad charge.

The buffalo broke his stance when the pellets from the second shot hit him. He turned west, threw his short tail up, and ran into the hills. Red disappeared over the rise after him.

Papa shook his head. "That Red," was all he could say. Papa knew Red was a mess sometimes, but every time he had ever needed him, Red had said, "Heck yes." That was worth a lot and covered a multitude of sins.

The cows had snorted a bit and turned a big circle but were too tired to rebel much. Papa turned a few back, and they held. He heard two more shots. One echoed in a canyon to the north.

Papa patted Bud and told him he was proud of him. Bud stamped, perhaps a little miffed he hadn't gotten in on the buffalo charge. Papa shared the feeling.

Nothing else to do, he pushed the cows further up the river into the black night. A half moon was up and it cast a soft light reflecting off the river and the mud.

He rode the silver streak and knew the cows were swishing through the grass ahead of him. Night hawks buzzed him with their wings and a screech owl started its nightly other-worldly argument.

He thought about Wilder and how for the second day in a row he was putting the boy at risk. Livy and Hank wouldn't like this. What if he was hurt in a canyon somewhere and about to die? He would never forgive himself, which was obvious, and he tried to dismiss the thought.

How do people forgive themselves?

He hadn't raised a boy before. He had raised Livy tough, but he hadn't put her in such situations, that he could recall. Maybe he had, on second thought, but he was young then and didn't realize the pain life could put you through. He shuddered.

But still, perhaps boys were different. Only a man could impart manliness to a man. He knew that. But what if a child died in the process? How far could you go? Where was the line between the danger, the risk, that made you what you were, and the danger that crushed you?

Papa knew he had been tested that way in the war. Then, death was a daily part of the equation. They did not get to draw lines to protect themselves. That was different. He hoped Wilder would never see war.

Riding slowly in the dark, he didn't recall his dad having these worries. All they did was work, and a lot of it was dangerous. But still, he knew of kids that died. The Russell boy, run over by a horse years ago. And the little girl . . . well, there were others that didn't survive the ranching childhood. All the fault of adults, too.

Was that going to be his destiny?

Papa made up his mind that he'd ride all night if he had to. He was going to die or find Wilder. That was all. He would gladly give his life for the boy. His life was about used up anyway, which was beside the point.

Red was waiting on a bluff up ahead, attempting to count cows in the moonlight. When Papa came abreast of him, Red rode down to meet him. They could see each other's shapes, but not features.

"I was waiting for the buffalo," Papa said.

"You won't be seeing him again."

"You killed him?" Papa couldn't believe that was true, but with Red anything was possible.

"No . . . nah, I didn't kill him. Just peppered the booger."

Papa nodded in the darkness.

"I've always wanted to do that, though."

"What, kill a buffalo?" Papa mused, "I have always wanted a robe, to be honest."

"Not kill one. Just shoot at something, riding full blast. Like in the movies. You haven't?"

"Maybe." Papa thought. "I guess so, when I was younger."

"Well, I got it out of my system. And it was kind of fun. And for a good cause, you know."

"Yeah, good cause, all right. They might put you in jail for shooting an official State of Texas buffalo."

"I just peppered him. He was depredating on my livestock. I was within my rights. Besides, I lost the murder weapon."

"You lost it?"

"Yup. You know how hard it is to jump gullies and pump a shotgun at the same time?"

"So you left it?"

"Couldn't find it."

"That's funny, Red."

"Yeah, I guess it is. It ain't as easy as the movie folks make it look."

They rode until they reached Rabbit. They swung down and read Wilder's note. That put them at ease for the moment, even though they knew the note was about eight hours old. Papa told Red he was going to ride all night to find him, but Red convinced him to get down and make a fire and eat and rest a bit before venturing off. Red would go with him, of course.

Papa nodded and Red put on the coffee.

They popped some meds recovered from the pack-saddle they removed from Rabbit. Red felt like being nosey.

"What do you take meds for?"

"I got a headache right now, but to be honest, Red, my prostate has been bad for years."

Red giggled.

"It ain't funny," Papa replied. "Chasing buffalos don't help it, either. What's killing you? Since we're being so honest here . . ."

"Well I've had hemorrhoids for 30 years. And high blood pressure. You're right, I don't recall ever sharing those juicy details with you."

"I guess not," Papa laughed at this new intimacy with a man he had known most of his life. "I'd just as soon be young again, if it weren't for all the nice surprises of getting old."

"You got that right," Red agreed with disgust.

"What's a hemorrhoid feel like?" Papa asked, trying to make a joke out of their misfortunes.

"Oh they're a joy to behold. Not quite a prolapsed uterus on a cow, but a little more than full arm palpitation," Red giggled. "That gets you in the ballpark."

The two old men laughed like they were junior high kids. Their pain eased and they forgot about it for a little while.

ᘉᘖ

CHAPTER THIRTEEN
One Word

After crackers and canned chili, which surprised Red since he was expecting Vienna sausages again, Papa and Red watched the fire and sipped coffee while their unsaddled horses grazed nearby. The smell of the low mesquite flames brought a peace they had known all their lives.

The coffee and hot food recharged them for the night ahead. Red said he'd move to Dallas for a Tums. He couldn't stop burping. Papa felt some heartburn creeping up, too. They decided they would find Wilder, sleep until sunup, and abandon the cattle. They could get them later. In some ways the drive had beaten them, but they were too old to care . . . much.

"That boy is all right, Wendell," Red said. "He's probably doing the exact same thing we're doing right now."

"He probably is. At least it's not raining and thundering."

"Yeah, that was no joke." Red paused. "You thought about Germany, didn't you? You think about the war much, after all these years?"

No one had ever asked Papa that question. Not Marian, not Livy, not Red. Hearing Red's question, Papa realized how much he would have liked to talk about it. But since no one had asked, he wasn't going to be the guy forcing his war stories on everyone. Red had been in the Pacific during the war, and they had swapped stories when they came home, like most vets, but it faded from their conversation before long. It never faded from their minds.

"From time to time. It's always there, I guess."

"Well, what do you think of the most?"

Papa was on unsteady ground, even with Red, who

seemed like he wanted to talk. Papa realized Red must have stories, too, that he wanted to tell. Wanted to tell them before they died with him.

Papa sipped his coffee and nodded to the fire.

"We were drinking coffee just like this, only not over a blue-smoke mesquite fire, of course. I don't know if it was December '44 or January '45. It was cold, and we were dug in half a mile from some little town in Germany. Ended with a 'dorf.'

"We never got warm. Never. I had known cold from panhandle winters but here, you know, we seldom had snow. And cold snaps end every couple of days, and we always had a house to go to. But that winter, we just lived in those foxholes. Smoking cigarettes and drinking coffee and scrounging for food. I've bought the best boots and wool socks I could afford ever since then. Just misery. Living like animals—no, much worse than animals.

"It was the Bulge, of course, and the Germans were everywhere. The brass was confused. Dorf wasn't occupied, as our Captain figured, and we were content to huddle in our holes when we could. There was no advance on our side. It was chaos. More than usual.

"Our whole battalion sat there watching that little town and hearing shelling off and on for a few days. Finally the Captain passed down an order to the Lieutenant and finally to our Sargent. We had to take a patrol into Dorf and fire our flares if we contacted the enemy.

"Patrols were suicide missions, as you know, especially with the Germans advancing with everything they had; tanks, infantry, artillery. We groaned, but our platoon of 12 had to go. Sarge ordered us to draw straws for two patrols. One would leave at eight p.m. and return at two a.m., when the other would leave.

Six short straws left at eight and six long at two. I got a long straw and went to sleep. It was stone quiet when they left into the woods.

"My six hours of sleep seemed like 30 seconds. All six guys returned, and we asked them what they saw. They said they didn't see anything, but that it was snowing hard. Sarge was with our group. We checked our gear, we had five Garands among us and a man with a BAR auto.

"We followed Sarge, who followed the first patrol's footprints in the snow. They were filling in from the fresh snow fall. We were heading into what felt like a maze of forest and field with little hope of finding our way back quickly if things went south. We came to the road into Dorf. Sarge whispered that the MLR (Main Line of Resistance) was just beyond the town. We crept down it in a line waiting for instant death as the snow fell around us. Visibility was 50 yards and we knew if we saw anyone it would be too close for anything but a fire fight. Suicide mission."

Red watched Papa, and Papa watched the fire, lost in his story.

"About three o'clock we could see Dorf through a short break in the storm, and Sarge saw some foxholes on the side of the road. He ordered us into them. We huddled and tried to cover up. The snow kept falling and covered us with seven or eight inches. It was cold, but we felt safe. Maybe that would be it, like the other patrol.

"At about six we heard gunfire and mortar shells exploding but didn't know where they were. We still hadn't accomplished our mission of making contact with the enemy. We had no information to bring back to the battalion. Sarge asked us, 'Who wants to go into Dorf?'

"My buddy Al Caparelli and I had discussed this eventuality, and we volunteered. I don't know why, I wasn't the volunteering kind, none of us were at that point, but we did it. We knew this was going to take us right to the enemy. It only made sense that the Germans were already in Dorf, with the MLR right behind the town. Maybe we owed those others guys from another patrol or something. It wasn't heroism. I can't remember.

"We got out of the foxhole and resumed the march down the road. Cap and me, side by side. I remember thinking that this was it, and it was kind of freeing, now that I recall it. I was walking to my death. I'd never be warm or see Texas again. I'd be frozen and full of bullet holes like so many others I had seen. But at least the worry was gone for a second."

Papa paused. Kicked log ends into the fire.

"Well, anyway. I was right. About 300 yards from Sarge and the foxhole in the down-pour snow we saw a line of Germans to our right in black uniforms. Fifty yards away. They were running toward Dorf. A machine gun was firing over their heads providing cover. 'Down, Cap!' I cried. We buried into the fluff of the snow-covered road, paralyzed with fear. We poked our heads up and dozens of Germans came out onto the road. My burst of bravery evaporated real quick.

"Cap whispered to me, 'Let's surrender.'

"I didn't have to think about it. I told him 'no' with as much force as I could risk. Germans were running parallel to us, not 15 yards away now. If they saw us we were sure we would be shot. We wouldn't have gotten off three rounds. I could almost smell those Krauts.

"I looked around and saw a hedge running along our side of the road. I thought we could make it and then have the woods to run to. I motioned my plan to Cap. We inched on our bellies through the deep snow, expecting at any second to hear German shouts and gunfire. My steel helmet burrowed through the snow, almost like a mole, and before we knew it we hit the ditch and then flopped over the hedge. We rested a minute, breathing like smoke stacks in the frigid air, and then poked our heads back over. The Germans were gone.

"We lay there and decided it was at least a company, between a hundred and two hundred men. They had the dark leather SS jackets we knew so well. We took off through the woods and crossed a field to the south where we knew Company I was dug in. On our run across the field four guys started chasing us. They weren't shooting, and we quickly figured out it was Sarge and the others.

"At Company I an intelligence officer interrogated us, and we told them about the company of SS soldiers. The officer said it must have only been a patrol and that we were just scared. What could we say to that? Of course, we had been scared, but it wasn't any patrol.

"We were proved right, because the next day that SS Mountain division attacked our battalion. We had high casualties. The day after that we advanced and I was back on the mortar and we took Dorf. A lot of men died on both sides. God, we destroyed that pretty little town."

Papa looked relieved to have made it to the end of the story.

"That night in the snow has never left me. What if I would have said 'yes' to Cap? We might have been shot. We might have spent the war in a prison camp. Or at least the next six months, as it turned out. I might not have known Marian. There'd be no Livy, no ranch, no grandson or granddaughter.

"We were so young. My whole life hinged on one word."

Red didn't know what to say. The story and the emotion woke up his own memories and feelings that he had known but pushed aside for 50 years. He'd tell his story someday. Not tonight.

"You need to tell Wilder that story," Red offered. It was the first time he'd said Wilder, instead of Wilber.

Papa shrugged. "What does it matter? Old men telling old stories."

But they both knew it mattered, even if they could lie to each other about it in the darkness.

CHAPTER FOURTEEN

Nobody Owns Me

Wilder didn't panic when he felt the wet licks on his face. Somehow he recognized the breath.

It was Coffee.

Wilder hugged the dog deeply and knew Papa must be close. He squeezed her in the low firelight and said "good dog" over and over again. He patted her with his good hand. His left was throbbing, but it was a good pain for the first time. It felt like a wound healing, now. And his pinky was no longer sticking out like a radio antenna.

Coffee licked him. Her whimpers sounded motherly to Wilder. He reached over and found the grape jelly from the breakfast in Turkey in his saddle bags. He peeled the tops back on two and held one out for Coffee, and they licked the sweet dark goodness together under the stars.

The moon was out, a little past half full, which was enough to make the pond shine. Wilder leaned back on his hands. He could see Fancy grazing. *What a great horse*, he thought. Things were looking up.

He put a few more sticks on the fire.

Then he jogged in the dark to the top of the dam and hollered, but Papa wasn't there. Wilder didn't think Coffee could have found him on her own, so he was surprised when he didn't see men or cattle as he looked down the canyon in the moonlight. He thought about wandering further but knew that would be ignorant. His camp was safe and would be until morning, and so he returned.

The mosquitos and buffalo gnats found him when he walked through the grass away from his fire, but he knew the solution for them. He found a big growth of horsemint and picked handfuls of the multi-tiered purple flower. He ground these up in his hands and rubbed the wet oil all over his clothes and face and ears. The warm citronella scent scattered the bugs quickly. Wilder was proud of this knowledge. Livy had showed it to him years ago.

Watching the fire, he heard what sounded like gun-shots in the distance, but he knew it could also be something with the oil locations. The oil tank batter-ies and wells that spotted the land were always mak-ing noise at all hours of the day and night. He wasn't really scared, but the loud bangs reminded him he had a pistol. He got it out and loaded five .45 rounds in the cylinder and let the hammer down carefully on the empty chamber, like he had been taught.

The pistol felt good in his hand. It was heavy and worn smooth. He wasn't sure if it still worked, since it looked to be at least a hundred years old. Wilder knew Colt pistols showed up around the Civil War and were used by Texas Rangers after that. It was one of those inventions that appeared for the first time with an almost perfect design. He pointed it at the moon and the water and thought about shooting it at a surfac-ing turtle's head, and then he put it down on his sad-dle blanket.

He roasted some of the Viennies on a stick. The lit-tle pink tubes bubbled and turned brown, then black, which made them edible. They weren't that far from hotdogs now. Wilder wished he had Tabasco. But he was starving and ended up eating the whole can of chicken, pig, and cow parts. It was a cowboy meal.

He had a horse, a dog, fire, and a good weapon. He guessed that was about all anyone needed.

He wrapped his pinky up tight to his index finger,

amazed that he had done the operation on his own and that it seemed to have worked right. The finger was tender as a sore tooth, and he had to unwrap it twice to get the right tension on the tape to allow for swelling but still keep it in place. His left hand immediately became usable again.

All that was left was sleep. He took another pull from his plum water and lay down on the blankets. Coffee had been waiting for the opportunity and she hobbled over to make her circle next to him. Wilder noticed how poorly she walked. Her back legs wobbled, and she was breathing heavy even after cooling down from her blind search.

His one fear in the night was tarantulas. He did not want to feel those ghastly legs on his body, his fingers, his face.

Wilder closed his eyes and listened to the cottonwood trees flutter above him. There wasn't much breeze, but the heart-shaped leaves didn't need much to start playing their water song. It wasn't a rustling sound like most trees, it was like small bells, click-clacking back and forth.

Wilder smiled, and then he heard the buffalo growl.

Wilder knew exactly what it was. The deep rumble of a sound buried in a living chest beneath mounds of muscle and bone and blood. Fear rippled through him. He knew the buffalo wasn't like a shark in a movie with an evil, personal agenda against people, but he understood the danger of all wild things. He was playing by the buffalo's rules now, on its home field. It demanded a level of respect that bordered on stark fear. Especially in the dark.

He knew if he heard it, then Fancy and the cows did, too. The sound was behind him in the canyon he had come up. He didn't reach for the pistol. He grabbed a log from the fire, circled the bottom of the pond, and looked over the dam. Coffee's ears were up, but she didn't charge off. She limped at his heels.

Wilder stayed close to the dam crest and peered over, shining the torch into the night. The bull was 30 yards off to the right, on a bluff looking down at Wilder. He was sweating and breathing hard. He looked nervous.

Wilder was scared of the beast and annoyed at his harassment of the cows, but he couldn't help but be awed by the animal. His black horns shone in the moonlight. The buffalo was like a movable mountain. Like a lord overseeing his kingdom.

Wilder crept toward him. At first he meant to shoo him away from his cows and his water hole, but then he was pulled toward the buffalo in curiosity, and perhaps veneration. He might never get this chance again.

The bull stared at him, unafraid. The torch blazed in the night between them.

Wilder crept closer, now foolishly away from the protection of the dam and the big elm at its base.

At ten feet, Wilder stood nose to nose with the buffalo bull. He could see red and yellow flame reflecting in its dark eyes nestled into its curly, dark wool. They stared at each other, just breathing.

Wilder saw the ear tags poking out, but they seemed much different than the tags domestic cows wore. They looked the same, but instead of a mark of ownership, they seemed ironic. *Nobody owns me*, the buffalo seemed to be saying, despite his plastic label. It occurred to Wilder that that was what wild meant.

He wondered why he had broken out. The park must have had ample feed and cows to breed. There certainly weren't going to be any buffalo cows anywhere else in Texas. Wilder knew the old bulls in Yellowstone became solitary. Why would they choose to live alone at the ends of their lives?

Wilder realized they were kind of like Papa.

Nobody and nothing will ever own me. I am my own.

The buffalo's growl, hoarse and low, seemed to make the ground unsteady at Wilder's feet. The boy came out of his trance and felt foolish. He muttered to himself—*mess with the bull, get the horns.* He respected the horns. He knew he was pushing the grace of this buffalo. He was pushing his wildness. He kept the torch high but backed away to the dam and back to his campfire.

He wasn't going to worry about the buffalo. He stoked up his fire, lay down with Coffee, and went to sleep.

There was another poem, and he would write it after he dreamed a little while.

Papa and Red hunted for the boy all night. They rode up and down the river, tracking by what they could see in the moonlight. Which was very little. The moon just wasn't bright enough for their old eyes to see tracks from horseback—or from the ground when they took a rest.

Neither had packed flashlights, which they recognized was a mistake. It was another detail added to the evidence that they weren't as able as they had once been. They rode for an hour at a time, keeping rough track of time by the movement of the moon, and met back at the campfire to compare notes and drink coffee and refuel with the granola bars that had begun to taste dry as horse oats.

At their four o'clock meeting they both fell asleep lying on the ground. Both men were played out and slumped over like they were dead. Bud and Burrito stood a few yards off from the fire, saddled, reins dropping to the ground. They grazed and, from experience, didn't break the reins as they trailed beside their hooves.

When the sky was morning-blue to the east and the mockingbirds, field larks, and bobwhite quail started talking, the men woke up. Papa was surprised and nervous. He rubbed his face and stood up, and then bent over. His body felt broken in ten places.

He gulped four aspirin and hobbled over to catch Bud, who was only 50 yards away. The reins were muddy and Papa cleaned them on his jeans. He tightened the cinch and told Bud he was sorry for leaving him saddled all night. Bud didn't reply.

Rabbit stared at him from his tie-up on the mesquite, stone-faced like usual.

Papa walked Rabbit and Bud to the river, they all drank, and Papa swung into the saddle on his third try. He walked the horse over the Red, who was adding fresh water to the all-night coffee pot. He added some fresh grounds to the black sludge at the bottom of the pot.

"Red, we gotta go," Papa said, as he tossed over Rabbit's lead rope so Red could tie him up again.

Red nodded. "I'll be right behind you. We should be able to track him now. We'll have him before the sun comes up."

Papa turned his horse to the west, up the river.

The tracks were clear now. They were the only ones who'd been in the pasture since the rain, and after two miles of tracking at a trot, Papa saw the hoof prints cross the river and head up the creek drainage. He saw cow tracks and one horse and a big buffalo print. A quarter mile up the canyon he smelled Wilder's campfire.

Papa loped through the canyon. He figured he should

have guessed this was where Wilder would go. It was close to where he left Rabbit. It was a good place to shelter. The cattle would probably stay put. *Someone taught this boy well*, he thought.

Papa saw the dam and then blue smoke as the sun was hitting the top of the canyon. He popped over the top of the dam and saw his grandson in his white underwear, sitting on Fancy bareback, in the middle of the dirt tank.

ꙴ

CHAPTER FIFTEEN

Toothpaste

Papa walked his horse down the dam face and spurred Bud into the water next to Wilder. The only thing Wilder wore besides the underwear was his belt, which held his knife. His eyes had been surprised and wide when he first saw Papa but had settled back into the narrow squint he had been trying to perfect.

"Congratulations, you survived. What are you doing now?"

"Just being a Comanche," Wilder replied, not missing a beat. He bashfully touched the medicine bag necklace that hung from his neck, across his widening chest. It held a tuft of Bluebonnet's black mane and a small tip of antler from Silverbelly, the mule deer he had killed last year on the ranch.

"You look about right. Are you a war party or just a lone brave?"

"Quanah took a vision quest somewhere around here. I guess that's what I've been doing."

Quanah Parker was the great chief of the Comanches, whose central homeland had been Palo Duro Canyon, not 30 miles away. Quanah was a fighter but then made friends with Colonel Goodnight when it was clear he could no longer win. Wilder had been reading about him all his life. His mother had been a white woman, Cynthia Ann, who was abducted by Comanches when she was nine. Wilder thought a lot about her, too.

"Did you get a vision?"

"Yes."

"Well."

"Can't say, Papa."

Papa nodded, as if he understood. Then he looked at Wilder's bandaged hand closely.

"What's that?"

"I pulled a cow from quicksand, and when I got her up she charged me. She missed, mainly, but her head popped my pinky out of place. The same one that popped out in a basketball game last year." Wilder paused and looked off at the few cows he could still see up the canyon.

"Is it still out?" Papa could see that it wasn't. Wilder was leading him along. He felt pretty proud of himself for his act of courage, setting the dislocated joint.

"Nope, it's back in."

"Hmmm . . . ," Papa murmured, impressed with the apparent grit as well. They both knew pain should be borne without complaint. The boy looked OK, so Papa let whatever parental instincts he once had to check out injuries fade.

Wilder thought Papa looked half dead. His whiskers were four days long and his eyes had deep, dark bags under them. He was dirty from head to toe. Papa looked around and walked his horse through the water over to Wilder's camp. He slid off his horse onto the shore like a dried-up leaf and Wilder watched him grimace as his first foot touched down.

Being too careful with the landing, Papa caught his left foot in the stirrup for a half second, which threw off his timing. He tumbled backward to the ground in a pile. Wilder heard the fall and watched in fear as Papa grunted with the impact. *Gosh, he looks terrible,* Wilder thought.

Papa lay there for a second, and Wilder knew he had to ignore it. He had to make it look like he hadn't seen. He turned Fancy in the pond and started walking her out the other side. He had never seen Papa fall like that before. There had been the ladder a few days ago, but that was different, the ladder had been bad.

How many spills can a 76-year-old man take? he wondered.

For Wilder's part, he felt as fresh and renewed as a spring calf. He was ready to ride, gather cattle, whatever. After he put his pants and boots back on.

But Papa unsaddled Bud, slid the saddle down, and propped it up on its horn. Then he lay down on his saddle blankets under the tree. Coffee poked his hand with her nose looking for affirmation, received it, and curled up next to Papa.

His hat off and his head propped up on his hands, Papa hollered across the pond to Wilder. Wilder got off Fancy and walked over to him barefoot in the mud.

"Wilder, I'm sorry again. We didn't stop looking for you. We looked for tracks all night but we couldn't see them."

"I figured that. I knew you wouldn't leave me."

"Well, still, I'm sorry. You did exactly right."

"Sorry for what? I had a great night. You didn't cause that buffalo to chase us. It wasn't your fault."

"Yeah, but you shouldn't have had to stay out here by yourself. A hundred things could have happened."

"But they didn't."

"They might next time," Papa said and rose up to look at Wilder. "It's a dangerous business. Most people don't understand that."

"I do."

Papa lay back down and closed his eyes. "Yes, I guess you do," he said.

"You can't protect me, Papa," Wilder said softly. The thought hadn't occurred to him until then. But it was true. He knew how to handle himself now. Wilder didn't know it, but Papa had said as much to Red last night.

"All you can do is make me strong."

Papa quit arguing. Maybe the boy was right.

The boy was right. Papa didn't know what to say, so he let his whipped body fall into sleep.

Wilder was itching to tell his stories about the quicksand cow, the buffalo, his pinky, and his first solo. He decided to leave off the first solo—it seemed a little juvenile to fish for compliments with that one—but he wanted to tell about the buffalo and the cow, at least. You could always talk about cows.

When Red crested the dam, Wilder exchanged funny looks with the old man. They held off any commentary about the other's appearance. Red looked beat, too. He saw Papa stretched out, and he soon had Burrito and Rabbit unsaddled and grazing. Red lay down under the cottonwoods near Papa.

Wilder swung back up on Fancy, still mostly naked. He had ridden bareback all his life, but always in a pen and with jeans and boots and spurs. Now he had the spirit of the buffalo in him and wanted to see what else he could do.

He kicked Fancy into a trot down the canyon to flatter ground, which hurt, but he soon found the rhythm of her gait. He gripped her mane hard and tried to ride with his back straight. His thighs seemed to meld into her back, like one continuous muscle that connected them. On a flat bluff he kicked her into a lope.

The wind on his bare chest blew the necklace into his face and then onto his back. With no hat pressing down his hair, he did not sweat. He and Fancy tore across the prairie grass in perfect unison. He hollered. He hollered at the grass and the wind and the sky and in return they whistled in his ears. He rode so fast his eyes watered and he let the drops stream past his cheeks and into his ears.

He wondered if Fancy could feel it. The connection that they had when all the cinches and saddles and spurs were gone. They were just two animals merging into one thundering unit. Something switched in Wilder's heart, but he didn't know what to call it.

Eventually he got sore, and his thighs were covered in Fancy's buckskin hair and sweat. His legs were dripping with their combined perspiration and he doubted he could hold on if they had to stop or turn fast. He reined her in, and they took the long way back in a slow walk.

The old men slept until just before noon, when Wilder had a lunch of fried summer sausage and potatoes ready for them. They drank coffee and boiled plum water.

Wilder had given Rabbit's back a good rub with dry grass. The burro stood still for him, without hobbles. Strangely, he hadn't grazed or drunk much water. Wilder figured desert animals had learned how to live on air. Stone-faced and doe-eyed, the burro just stared back at him.

While the old men slept, Wilder scratched out a few lines of his poem. He wrote them in the saddlebag poetry book Mrs. Brann had given him at school.

Buffalo fire burns to be free
Burns the grass and burns the tree—
Burned out of the cow
won't burn out of me.

And then he made a few notes on the horses drinking.

Tired horses drink
from a windmill's pump
water runs down their chest and legs
things creak connected

I must remember,
I must remember.

His poems were just notes. Mrs. Brann had taught him to find beauty and make notes about it. After a while he found that he was always thinking about poetry and was excited when he found some lying around a pasture.

He folded the buffalo wool he had picked up into the pages. He knew it would have to go on his medicine necklace in some way. Maybe he could make a pouch. His medicine was growing and he was pleased.

"Wilder, we're going to leave the cows," Papa announced when they had finished their plates. Red looked at the fire.

Wilder looked at him funny, not wanting to be disrespectful but completely surprised at the words.

"We can get these cows in a few days. I think Red and I have had our fill of fun."

Wilder paused, not wanting to blurt out something foolish. If Papa was talking about giving up he must have a good reason. But nothing in Wilder was ready to quit.

"How far are we from Red's ranch?" Wilder asked.

Red spoke up, "Not far, just one more pasture to cross after this one," Red said. "Maybe five miles."

"Haven't we got to ride out of here anyway?" Wilder asked.

Papa and Red had realized that when they made the decision. But a slow walk to the gate was a much different thing than gathering the cows again with a rogue buffalo in the mix.

"We do. But we might just be a little too beat up to finish right now. We'll get them with trailers in a few days." Papa certainly didn't want to get into all the health problems he and Red had and how the two men would be healing up with a week of doctor visits after this deal. The truth was, Red and Papa probably could have finished, but Papa felt guilty about what he had put Wilder through. He was relieved they were all OK and didn't want to push his luck any further. Of course, he wasn't going to blame it on Wilder out loud.

Wilder wanted to argue. He was worried about the two old men, not himself. He knew he could make it, but he didn't know about them. Like Papa, he would never say that.

So they all three sat there pitying the others and canceling the drive in their minds. That was the only solution. They all felt the sour stomach of defeat.

Red got up, dusted off his pants, and wandered over to catch Burrito.

"The buffalo came in last night," Wilder said to Papa.

"Oh really? What happened?"

"I heard him grunting below the dam, and I walked out to him with a torch." Wilder relayed the experience, and Papa's eyes twinkled as he relived Wilder's night. He wondered if this was the "vision" Wilder had mentioned or a real event. Either way, it was a good one.

They sat together under the elm as the cook fire burned low and the day started to feel hot again.

"Isn't that why we came out here?" Wilder said.

"It is," Papa agreed, knowing what Wilder was getting at.

"Something else good might happen."

"But something bad might, too. Wilder, you've got to understand, this lifestyle doesn't make a lot of sense. I can't keep risking your life for something that just isn't necessary.

"A desk job someday is your best bet, and if not

that, quit the horses and ropes and just farm cattle like those other guys." Papa couldn't believe what he was saying. He was lying to the boy. But he didn't feel like he had any other options.

"Why didn't you do that?" Wilder cornered him, unsure of where this conversation would go.

Papa rubbed his old hands together. The yellowed calluses made a scratching sound that Wilder's hands never did. He didn't want to answer the question but figured he had to. And it was something he had thought about before.

"I don't know. I love the land I guess. And maybe that's because it never got boring. Some things are beautiful as they are and can't be continuously improved. Like a saddle, or a rope, or grass after a rain. The relationship you build with a horse. But all those things can kill you, too. They are valuable because they are hard.

"Horses should have been obsolete a hundred years ago. But we're still out here risking our necks on them. I don't know why. You have to kind of like being an old fool to do it. To be honest, cowboying is a grand foolishness."

"Why can't I do the same thing?" Wilder asked.

"Cause you might die in the process."

"I feel like I'm getting stronger."

Papa laughed, "I know, that's the problem with cowboys. They've got too much *boy* in them."

Wilder was beaten. He was on the cusp of being disrespectful and he knew it. If they had to quit the drive, he knew he would be the unspoken scapegoat. He wouldn't push his case, though; he had a hunch that quitting was about the old men being old men.

"Well, Papa, I'll do whatever you say, of course, but I want you to know I've got some left."

"Some what?"

"Some toothpaste."

"Toothpaste?"

"You told me once that life was like a toothpaste tube. You want to make sure you use it all up."

"I said that?"

"Yes. Even when the tube seems like it is all gone, if you keep squeezing and squeezing and roll the thing up, there's always a little more. I can get a week out of a tube Molly is done with."

Did Papa have any left? That's the question Wilder rolled around in his head. Did Red?

Red came back to the fire to get his blankets and saddle. Their decision had certainly dampened his cheery personality.

Papa stood up and Wilder followed.

"The boy here says he can make it." Papa said it like it was a gauntlet being thrown down before them.

Red's eyes flashed. "He does?"

Wilder looked down, not wanting to be showy in front of his elders. Just honest. He would go along with whatever they decided.

"He does," Papa finished.

"Well, I can sleep when I'm dead, I guess," Red answered. "That'll be soon enough."

Wilder smiled. He started clearing camp while Papa caught their horses. As they all swung up ten minutes later, Wilder had the thought that every time you got on a horse it was an act of courage.

As they moved up the canyon to find the cows, for the first time, Wilder led.

ᘜ

CHAPTER SIXTEEN

Dinosaurs and Cowboys

It was hard riding for a couple hours to gather the herd. Wilder's bunch had stayed within a mile radius up and around the canyon. They gathered and herded to the river without any problems other than the constant up and down elevation and brushy work of canyon pastures. Their horses had lathered up quickly.

At the river, Wilder tied Rabbit to a tree on the backside of the herd. He followed Red and Papa out in a big circle to find the rest of the cows. Wilder had the most riding to do, since he had to get to the rear of the herd somehow and take back up the drag. He spurred Fancy over bluff after bluff until he was sure he was past any retreating cows. The buffalo was gone.

Slowly, Wilder and Papa and Red appeared with little bunches of cows and merged them into one herd heading west again. It was the first real riding Wilder had gotten to do, and he and Fancy both leaned into the work. Wilder wanted to rope something and shook out a loop. He rode along swinging his twine at bunch grass and sage.

They found Rabbit and the other cows, and two or three starving calves reunited with their mothers with bawls and licks. The riders watched them join back up before pushing them. Wilder led Rabbit again. The burro moved like a walking statue.

It was only two miles to the end of the massive pasture. When they saw the fence line, Papa eased ahead like always to open the gate. The cows worked through, and finally they were finished with the worst of their ordeal. Red took a count as the cows went through the gate and Wilder got down to close it. Papa and Red joined him on the ground, and Red said they had all the calves and were missing two cows. The four-wheeler cowboys would pen the two cows and he'd get them in a trailer tomorrow. No big deal.

It was hot now, at three o'clock. They tightened their cinches and drank water.

Coffee came hobbling up, limping worse and panting hard. Her toothpaste tube was getting low. Papa and Wilder both looked at her with concern.

"The next pasture after this one is home, boys." Red announced what they all knew. "Maybe two miles to the gate. I bet Art will be looking for us and help us bring them in."

They were all relieved and also little ashamed they had doubted the wisdom of finishing. Papa and Red were sore with bruises. Their legs had been rubbed raw in multiple places, then scabbed over at night, and rebroken open each day. The oozing sores welded to their jeans as sweat and blood seeped out and then dried throughout the day. Instead of getting stronger from the work and exposure, they had gotten weaker. Their prime long past, they made it through on stubborn perseverance.

Drinking the river water hadn't helped either. Both men had made secret trips to the bushes since morning.

Wilder was the opposite. He was ready and willing to take the cows to Montana. He wanted to ask Papa to swap positions with him, flank for drag, but kept quiet.

"I guess we lost that buffalo," Wilder wondered, a bit sad that that part of the adventure was over.

"Yeah, I'll call that in when we get back," Red replied. "I won't be offering to join in the roundup."

"How will they catch him?" Wilder wondered.

"With a thirty ought-six most likely," Papa said.

"That's true, they'll have to tranq him," Red said. A gun with a tranquilizer dart was the only way to handle an animal like that in open country, the old men knew. There wasn't a horse or a man that could hold a bull like that. Wild things had to be either drugged or killed to make them go along with civilization.

"Speaking of guns, Mr. Guffey, what happened to old Stubby?" Wilder asked. He had noticed Red's saddle scabbard was empty.

"I donated it."

"To what?"

"The Panhandle Plains Museum in Canyon."

"How did you do that?"

"Oh, I left it out here for an archeologist to dig up someday. When they're studying the old tales about when people used to ride horses and herd cattle. There'll be an exhibit that reads, 'Dinosaurs and Cowboys: What in the Sam Hill Happened Here?'"

Red cackled at his joke. Papa smiled.

Wilder smiled, too, and nodded and let it go. He had learned Red was more likely to grow wings and fly than give a direct answer to something. Maybe Papa would tell him later.

They mounted up and thought about Red's wife, Mary, and the iced tea and hot rolls and roast and brown gravy they would have at her table in a few hours. Of course, she probably had the same meal ready last night, when they were supposed to show. Red's house would be cool and the chairs soft.

As they remounted, Wilder gathered up Coffee and cradled her in his arms. He could barely manage it, but he pulled himself into the saddle and draped the dog across the front of the seat behind the horn. Fancy didn't seem to mind, and Coffee was willing.

He was near useless for cow work now, dragging

Rabbit and holding Coffee in balance. It was worth it. The job was done. He could take care of the old dog and bump up the cows for two miles.

They soon had the cows bunched back up and headed west. The canyons on either side of the river grew steeper, and the cottonwood groves at the bottom were thicker. Sometimes they rode though what felt like forest. The river bottom narrowed in places, but the water level never rose. Cedars hadn't been cleared in this pasture, or more likely they couldn't be cleared by the standard method of a bulldozer. The land was too steep.

The land was more like Papa's ranch, now. It had pasture land in the rough canyon bottoms and grazing on top of the caprock on the vast Llano Estacado. For thousands of years erosion had broken boulders off the cap and they had rolled down, leaving crumbling monuments to water and wind. The rocks had been seafloor at one point, and Wilder imagined he was riding through a reef with sharks and stingrays all around.

Wilder rode past a buzzard tree, occupied by an assembly of the red-faced birds that stared back at him. White splotches of dried droppings lined the dead cedar's limbs. The birds didn't spook, just looked at him like he was lunch as he rode by at 20 yards. He had been as close to buzzards as he needed to be, for a lifetime.

Finally Wilder saw the home fence ahead. There was a windmill spinning on the other side and Wilder figured he would throw himself and Coffee right into the tank. Red moved to get the gate this time, since it was closest to him on the north side of the river, which was where his ranch lay. Wilder saw a mule deer doe near to the windmill.

The cows seemed to understand and funneled

through the gap. They trotted into the pasture and kept going until they arrived at the windmill in the foothills. Wilder let out a whoop when the last calf ran through.

Red closed the gate and groaned as he pulled himself up into the saddle for what surely would be the last time. The cows circled the big, rusted-red steel tank. Knee-high green grass waved in the breeze.

Red and Papa smiled at the sight.

"Well, that was easy," Red said with a big grin.

"Yeah . . . easy as she goes," Papa added.

Wilder slid off his seat and half dropped, half eased Coffee down to the ground. She panted and it looked like a smile. She seemed to know she was home.

"Now we just have to go help Art finish hauling hay. He would have met us if he'd have been done."

Papa chuckled, amused at the absurd statement.

"When I see you lift a bale . . ." Papa said.

"OK, fine, you and Wilder go to town and get us some Allsup's burritos for dinner, and I'll be bucking bales."

Wilder knew this was nonsense. He did like Allsup's fried burritos, though. An ice cold Dr Pepper sounded like something too good to be true. He was almost there.

After the cows drank, they moved their horses up to the tank for their turn. Wilder walked Fancy up and considered jumping in the cool water. He put his hand in the stream from the well pipe and smelled the water. It smelled a little like metal, as it should. He rubbed his fingers together and the wind blew the chill into his body. He drank deep and came up dripping.

Coffee had wandered off. He wanted to toss her in so she could get a drink, although he knew heelers didn't usually like to swim, but she had disappeared.

He walked Fancy to the runoff pond full of bullfrogs and algae and stood on the edge to look for her.

In the tall grass behind the dam he saw Coffee with her nose down and ears up. She was tracking something in the grass. The small dog could hardly be seen in the Johnson grass and the tall purple-headed basket flowers that grew in the wet ground. Wilder watched her, figuring she had found another snake.

She vanished into the grass and Wilder let her go. Several yards in front of her, he saw something move. It moved slow, like a porcupine. It was brown and white and didn't seem to be spooked. It wasn't Coffee.

It was a spotted fawn. The deer couldn't have been a day or two old and was no bigger than a house cat. It walked out of the tall grass, and Coffee nosed up to its short fluffy tail with a small black tip. It was a mule deer with huge ears poking out from its head. The deer opened its tiny black mouth and bleated. It was a soft cry for its mother.

Coffee wasn't attacking the fawn. The old dog had certainly come across dozens like it in her lifetime on the ranch. She was just interested, as all dogs are in new things. Wilder had the same initial impulse as the dog. He wanted to check it out. The baby deer was gorgeous and begged to be petted and held.

He knew better, however, and held his ground. The fawn continued to bleat and wandered a few steps down the hill toward the river. It looked like it was panting in the heat.

From the corner of his eye, Wilder saw movement that wasn't a big black cow. He focused on it and knew it was the mama doe. She was a mature doe, about 150 pounds, close in size to a three-year-old buck, Wilder figured. She emerged from a hackberry motte to the west with her head up and ears erect.

Wilder was amused, *This is going to be interesting.* Papa and Red were still at the windmill behind him but had noticed the doe coming up.

The doe stepped toward her fawn from about 50 yards away with a deliberate stiff-legged march. Then she made a snort-wheeze sound, loudly. Wilder knew those were warning sounds. The fawn angled back toward her. Wilder could see the doe's swollen milk bag under her rear flank. Coffee kept sniffing.

At 30 yards the doe charged.

"Oh no," Wilder muttered.

Before he could holler "Coffee!" the doe was on her. She rose up on her hind legs and began pummeling the short dog with her front hooves. Coffee must not have heard her coming and was taken by surprise. She was immediately turned on her belly by the strikes and took rapid-fire blows beneath the doe.

Wilder dropped the reins and grabbed the pistol from his saddle bags. He spun the cylinder as he ran and cocked the hammer back.

"Coffee, no girl! No!!!" he yelled, to no avail. Coffee couldn't do anything to defend herself. Wilder was in shock at how fast the sleek doe had turned into an animal of fury.

The fawn stood ten feet away from the dust and tumble of the fight, staring off into the distance, panting.

Wilder neared the battle with the pointed the pistol and yelled as loud as he could. He found the doe in the sights of the pistol . . . and he knew he couldn't shoot.

The doe stopped and stood panting over the dog. She stared at him.

Wilder raised the pistol sights ten feet over her head and fired.

Boom!

The pistol bucked in his small hands and surprised him with the incredible sound.

The doe turned and he fired over her head again. The pistol sound and smell filled the canyons and echoed back and forth. The gray gunsmoke rose up from the barrel in the stillness and then, like the doe, was gone.

Papa and Red had moved their horses toward Wilder but were too late to make a difference.

The fawn stood breathing hard, bewildered at what had just happened in its young life. Then it lay down in a clump of dried Indian blankets, seeming exhausted.

Coffee was down in a heap in the trampled grass. She didn't move.

ᗯᑫ™

CHAPTER SEVENTEEN
Short Lives

Wilder made it clear he would carry the dog back to Red's place.

They had all gotten down and checked her wounds. There wasn't one big gash anywhere. One eye was shut and oozing. She was bruised and bleeding all over and breathing like a whisper.

Wilder cuddled her with both arms as he sat in the saddle. He had tied his reins together around Fancy's neck. Holding Coffee was harder now, since she was completely limp and his left hand was still swollen and sore, but it was bearable. He had to readjust a few times. He rode the mile and half to Red's house without reining. Fancy followed in the tracks of Bud and Burrito and Rabbit who were leading the procession.

By the time they reached the barn, Coffee had stopped breathing. She was loose in Wilder's arms, and Papa took her and laid her in the back of his pickup. Art had retrieved his truck and trailer for him from Turkey.

They loaded their horses in the trailer and made some small talk with Red's wife, Mary, when she came out to greet them.

"You men smell like a dead skunk," she said sweetly, knowingly. Wilder liked that she said "men," referring to all of them.

"You must be smelling a dead skunk under the barn, darling," Red said, "cause it couldn't be us. Well, maybe Wilber, he did some outhouse plumbing a while back."

Papa seemed to look at her longingly for a second, as he tipped his hat to her. He remembered coming home to a good woman. A beautiful woman that softened your sharp edges and made you more than you were. Better.

Wilder helped Red take the pack saddle off Rabbit and lead him to the pens. The burro still looked at them stone-faced, seemingly indifferent to his lot in life. He had done his job admirably and was somehow still alive. Wilder patted him and told him thanks.

It was seven o'clock and, while Wilder was sad, he was also hungry and knew they needed to eat together and then go home. He put a good face on it. They all did. It wasn't the time to grieve Coffee. Which seemed harsh to Wilder, but he knew it was true.

During the meal, Wilder and the men put the dog and deer accident behind them and did their best to recount their adventure to Mary. She oohed and ahhed over them with a wry ranch-wife smile and refilled their iced teas when needed. The house was cool and the chairs soft, as expected. The food was a revelation and they all ate like starving soldiers. Mary didn't mention that she had cooked the big meal twice. She had given the first meal to Art and his family.

Outside in the dusk, Red handed Wilder a stiff blue check. Wilder folded it without checking the amount and slid it into his back pocket. He didn't know yet that the old man had forgotten and written "Wilber Good" on the check. Or that it was for 450 bucks.

"What's this for, Mr. Guffey?" Wilder asked.

"Cowboy day work. The going rate."

"I figured we were just neighboring. You don't have to pay me."

"Ha, don't be silly, son. You almost died, two, maybe three times. That's cowboy work. Which they really ought to just call hazard pay. Kind of like the military."

"Well, thanks for having me. Will you tell Art thanks for the goat jerky? It got me through."

"Yup, and I'll pay Wendell back by gracing him with my presence at his next branding."

Papa turned to leave, saying "See ya, Red."

"See ya, Wendell," he replied and went into the house.

Nobody mentioned the dead dog in the truck bed.

It was only 15 minutes to Papa's ranch, the Tree Water. Wilder looked at Coffee's paw prints on the center console between them. He fingered some of the dried mud and then stopped when he broke some off. He wanted it to last.

They were all talked out and worked out and the tiredness caught up with them in one big pile that suffocated them into slow movements and groans. At the ranch, they unsaddled the horses and put their gear away in the dark.

Wilder stayed out in the night with Fancy and Bud, just to watch them roll. Their backs and sides were dark with sweat and grime. All their burdens gone, the task finished, they knelt down and celebrated in the dirt. Fancy couldn't go all the way over to catch both sides anymore; she rose up after doing one side and then rolled on the other.

Wilder saw Coffee's body on the fireplace stone work when he went inside. Papa had laid her there for the night.

Wilder looked at his white pearl snap shirt in the bathroom mirror before taking it off. It was black in places, and red. Coffee's blood. He was too tired to cry. He had cried too much at death. He recalled Bluebonnet and Silverbelly. Maybe he was hardened now, like Papa. He wasn't sure if that was what he wanted to be or not.

Brown water ran off his body for several minutes. He watched it drain on the white tub bottom where it would run out of the house and into the cess pool, and back to the Earth where they had collected it.

He slept like a dead man.

Papa moved like an old, old man the next morning. He shuffled his feet some on the wood floor in his socks. He took some aspirin with his coffee and toast and decided to stay in the house. He needed his body to start working again before Wilder saw him. It was the first time in 14 years he hadn't had morning coffee with his dog.

He was spread out in his easy chair when Wilder got up at ten a.m.

Papa put the foot rest down and rocked the chair a few times to propel himself up and out of the deep cushions.

"Let's go do our little chore," he said to Wilder, and Wilder knew what he meant. Wilder scooped up Coffee from the fireplace. She was stiff and cold. Wilder knew that was coming and had steeled himself against it, but a few tears leaked out. He wiped them. *Why does death have to be so ugly*, he thought.

They got shovels and drove as close as they could to the burial plot they had visited before the trip. The place in the trees that held Marian and Josephine.

"We gonna bury her inside the fence, with people?" Wilder asked before starting his carry.

"Yeah, why not? I don't figure I'll be around to bury any more dogs," Papa replied.

"Are there other dogs in there?"

"Well, not in there, no. I've buried lots of dogs on this ranch, though. That's the only problem with a dog. Short life."

Papa carried the shovels and Wilder carried Coffee

up the rise to the grove that held the cemetery. They went inside the black gate with the two markers and Wilder laid Coffee down.

"She was Marian's dog, too," Papa said.

"Did she like dogs?"

"Sure, she loved dogs. Marian picked up Coffee in Verbena one day when she was getting her hair done. I was surprised. It was about the time your mom told us she was pregnant with you."

"You named her, though."

"I guess so. Names come and go with animals, it seems. When one dies you get so you don't want to name them anymore. But then you do. For something silly, usually. For something you love . . . like Coffee."

Papa picked a spot at the back of the enclosure, and it didn't take long to dig in the wet ground. They went deep, knowing that a coyote might hop into the enclosed area and do some digging. They laid the beautiful spotted blue coat of Coffee in the ground and gave her back to the soil. Wilder patted the place down with his shovel and carried some rocks from outside the pen to stand guard over her.

They sat down gently with all the accumulated soreness of the past three days and leaned back against the black steel bars of the fence. There wasn't anything to be in a hurry about.

Wilder looked at Papa's marker in front of him. He saw the blank spot next to Papa's birthday again. It was just so strange to him. He wondered what date it might read some day. What would Wilder's second date be?

"You're going to be a heck of a hand at whatever you choose to do in life. You did a good job on the drive."

Wilder nodded. "You, too."

Papa chuckled. "Maybe. I think me and Red found something out about ourselves on that little deal."

"What?"

"I think you know," Papa mused. "Something about how much toothpaste we have left, but we don't need to say it out loud."

"We didn't die."

"No, not yet."

"Why do you always say it like that?"

"I thought we went through that. That little blank spot over there next to my birthday. It's already filled in. It's just that not you or me or anyone else knows it yet."

"How about ten more years?"

"Ten more years? That's a long time."

"Another toothpaste secret is," Wilder explained, "you can cut the tube open and get another couple days out of it. Don't waste nothing. Just have the shell to throw away.

"Sunny and I will be married by then. We'll have some babies and you can drag them out here and talk gloom and doom to them. Wise them up about being an old fool."

And that was the happiest thought Papa had had in a long time. He could see it. The vision cracked his heart open a bit. He passed a tear or two, but Wilder didn't notice. Wilder could hear the cottonwoods and the cicadas. An ant crawled across his leg and he brushed it off. A field lark sang.

They stood up and started for the gate and the pickup, each with a shovel in their hand. Green grass swished against their legs. Wilder stopped to open the gate and said, "Papa, I sure have seen a lot of death on this ranch."

"Yeah, but you've seen an awful lot of life, too."

They didn't look back or go to the cemetery the rest

of the summer. Wilder knew not to be sad about Coffee anymore.

It had been a good death.

The End

ᘜ

APPENDIX

Last Will and Testament of Wilder Good

I don't know how Wills work, but I am writing this one down in case I don't survive this drive. I guess I don't own much, now that I think about it.

I give my saddle to Molly. It was Momma's and it should be hers now. She can have all my horse gear, too. She will need it someday. Tell her I love her.

I have $367 in a can buried near the raccoon tree in the backyard. There's a big chunk of obsidian on the ground over the spot. I give this money to Momma to buy a new pair of custom cowboy boots from Beck's in Amarillo. She can have my brand put on the front but she doesn't have to. I know she's wanted really good boots for a long time. Tell her I love her.

I give my Winchester .270 to Dad. It needs to stay in the family and he needs a gun with some scratches on it to kill elk. Tell him I love him.

I give my elk head to Gale, but he won't want it. Just offer it to him. Tell him I love him.

I give my backpack and camping gear to Big. He needs a real pack, and he needs to remember all the stuff I taught him last month for the rest of his life. Punch him for me.

I give my tomahawk to Corndog. He liked it. Punch him for me.

I give my medicine bag to Sunny. (If that is OK with Momma and Dad.) It hung close to my heart, like her. Tell her I love her.

Main Point—Do not blame Papa for my death. He'll take this awful hard. I wanted to go on this trip and understood the dangers. Accidents happen in wild country and I hope to have died with a smile on my face under a bright sun.

I will see you all shortly. None of us are here very long.

ACKNOWLEDGMENTS

Many thanks to the team at Paul Dry Books in Philadelphia—Paul, Julia, Will, Mara. It's a great joy to make nourishing literature for children with all of you. I am grateful to all of you for believing in the Wilder stories. America is such a big country. I am proud that Philadelphia and Texas can collaborate in this way.

Thanks again to Cliff Wilke and Jerry Shelton for the chapter and cover art. Where would the books be without you guys? Your friendship and art are reward enough for writing a book.

Thanks to the early manuscript readers of this book—Justin Brown, Sheila Delony, Max Chance, Billy Hughes, and Dad. Special thanks to the most important first readers of everything I write, my kids and wife. I write for you always—SLAJHJ.

Thanks to my old Greek and Torah professor, mentor, and friend—Dr. Steve Eckstein. He lived the WWII story from the Battle of the Bulge that Papa tells Red in Chapter 13. He gave me permission to use the story, and even told me "thanks," and then went home to be with the Lord later in the year—98 years old.

Thanks to all the Wilder Good readers and fans that buy the books and are not content to live a sedentary life watching screens. Those who love clothes that smell like campfire smoke, watching deer that don't see them, and long days covered in dirt and smiles and sunlight. I'm right there with you.

Thanks to all the old men that raised and taught

me about the land and how to be a man in Roosevelt County: Wendell Best, Tommy Goff, Clarence Thompson, Nelson Rector, Alvis Griffith, and my Papa, Jack Paysinger. How fortunate I was to grow up watching and listening to you in turned-off pickups on dirt roads, at cattle brandings, around big meals, and in small church buildings.

From a Bend in Bethel
for my Roosevelt County heroes

He stood a little crooked
in a straight-backed country
where we looked at the sun
rise over cattle backs and coyote tracks.
Like the Siberian elm,
he was drought-resistant
and tolerated poor soil
and cast a shade on hot days
that covered many.
We grew in his shelter,
his kindness,
his eyes soft like a cottontail's
his speech like a mother cow
over her crying calf.
Gentle, gentle, always gentle—
as a young boy I saw that strong man cry
and I never forgot.

So, I will remember
to sing the anthem
of those that came before me—
the good men of the Lord and the land.

ABOUT THE AUTHOR

S. J. Dahlstrom lives and writes in West Texas with his wife and children. A fifth-genera-  tion Texan, Dahlstrom's *Wilder Good* series has won the Wrangler Western Heritage Award twice, the Will Rogers Medal- lion four times, finalist for the Lamplighter Award three times, and twice a Spur finalist from the Western Writers of America.

Interested in all things outdoors and creative, he writes poetry while bowhunting and collects wild- flower seeds when doing ranch work. He lives by the twin mottos "Be Wilder" and "Find Beauty" and is hap- piest when he doesn't have to comb his hair.

S.J.'s writing draws on his experiences as a cow- boy, husband, father—and as a founder of Whetstone Boys Ranch. He says, "I wrote these stories about Wilder Good for kids who grew up in the outdoors and for kids who long for the outdoors . . . working, fish- ing, hunting, farms, ranches, mountains and prairies. We should not forget that we have real adventure to offer kids, if we can have the courage to turn off our machines and screens and go outside."

You can learn more about S.J. Dahlstrom and *The Adventures of Wilder Good* series at www.wildergood. com.

Coming Soon!

#8

THE ADVENTURES OF WILDER GOOD

HEARTWOOD MOUNTAIN